12/12/1985

The Gift Horse

Into the ring cantered the ugliest horse Kelsie had ever seen. He was a big raw-boned skewbald, goose-rumped and cow-hocked. There was nothing that could be said in favour of his appearance. His head was too large and his eyes too small. His gait was awkward and he tossed his head all the time as he completed a lap of the ring.

'Pinto stallion, my foot!' Toby was disgusted. 'It's a common old skewbald gelding, and an evil looking brute at that.' The music stopped with a crash of the drums as the skewbald came to a halt in the centre of the ring with a spectacular rear and a neigh that echoed round the tent.

D0611120

THE GIFT HORSE

Alexa Romanes

Beaver Books

For Tamzin, Polly and Bryher

A Beaver Book
Published by Arrow Books Limited
17–21 Conway Street, London W1P 6JD

An imprint of the Hutchinson Publishing Group

London Melbourne Sydney Auckland
Johannesburg and agencies throughout the world

First published 1985

© Alexa Romanes 1985

This book is sold subject to the condition that it shall not, by way of trade or otherwise, be lent, resold, hired out, or otherwise circulated without the publisher's prior consent in any form of binding or cover other than that in which it is published and without a similar condition including this condition being imposed on the subsequent purchaser.

Set in Linoterm Baskerville
by JH Graphics Limited, Reading

Made and printed in Great Britain
by Anchor Brendon Ltd
Tiptree, Essex

ISBN 0 09 943750 3

Contents

The author would like to thank Pat Burgess of the Wilton branch of the RDA and Sally Garnett of the Broughton branch for their advice and encouragement.

1

Return to Crantock

Being on the short side, Kelsie could only see the top of her mother's head from her position at the back of the group of people clustered on the church steps. Ellen Forbes was wearing a rose-petal hat in a violent shade of pink and next to it was the balding head of the groom. Kelsie groaned softly and shifted from foot to foot. The coat she had been hastily bundled into was hot and uncomfortable and the little velvet hat skewered on one side of her curly red head was plain ridiculous. The whole situation was ridiculous.

Someone called out 'What about the confetti?' and immediately two people dashed forward with little boxes and a shower of coloured paper was thrown over the bridal pair. Kelsie's mother ducked and giggled as photographers jostled and called out for them to 'look this way, please'.

Kelsie supposed her mother was enjoying it, but she was beginning to regret having got herself involved in this showbiz publicity stunt. At lunch-time the director had informed them that there was to be a photo call for the press that afternoon, and that at the same time a special wedding line-up would be taken for the front cover of the *TV Times*.

'Yes, the front cover, folks! It's not every day that

the stars of the nation's most popular TV series get married.' Then he had put an arm round Kelsie's shoulders. 'And since we have the blushing bride's charming daughter with us, why don't we put you in the picture too? Wardrobe'll find you something to wear . . .'

So one of the wardrobe girls had found her the hideous coat and hat – in the obscurity of the back row no one should notice her worn jeans and trainers – and she had submitted herself to the attentions of the make-up department. That was bad enough, but then they'd had to stand for ages in front of this country church, with what seemed like the whole village watching, while press photographers took shots from every angle. In the road behind them, the TV company's technicians were assembling their equipment. At last a tall man who Kelsie had learned to refer to as the Production Manager, shouted out above the hubbub of journalists, actors, technicians and bystanders.

'OK, everybody, that's it! We must get on with the recording now. The road is only closed to traffic until four o'clock, and we've got several scenes to get through.'

Thankfully Kelsie nipped out from the back row, unpinning the velvet hat as she went. It was a warm spring afternoon and she was glad to get out of the coat and to hand the clothes over. She crossed the road for a view of the wedding group as they came out of the church, this time for the benefit of the TV cameras.

Kelsie had spent nearly a week with the cast and crew of 'Pringle's Parish', Midway Television's long-running soap opera. Her mother Ellen Forbes had joined the series less than a year ago, but her character, a lively, warm-hearted district nurse, had proved so popular that not only had she been given a long-term contract but the scriptwriters had married her off to the main character, Peter Pringle, the vicar. Kelsie hadn't seen her mother since Ellen had come to Cornwall at Christmas, so she had made the long journey to Manchester for this special occasion.

'I shall be working most of the time,' Ellen had written, 'but you can come on the set during the day, and we'll have our evenings together. There will be a big party to celebrate 'The Wedding'. (Any chance of you having anything other than jeans or jodhpurs to wear? If not, I'll buy you something while you're here. In all the shops Manchester has to offer, there must be *one* dress you'd like!) I think you'll find the set and locations interesting, and lots of people here want to meet you. I know how busy you are with the horses and studying and helping Jean with the riding school, but do try to come. I'm sure you'll enjoy it once you're here. A change is as good as a rest they say!'

Certainly nothing could be more different from her present life in Cornwall, thought Kelsie, as the actors rehearsed walking out of the church for the fourth time. At Crantock so much was crammed into every day that not a single minute was wasted. Here – well, she supposed they were all busy in their own strange way – there were always people who seemed to be just standing about, and it took so long to rehearse and record such short scenes.

Suddenly, the church bells rang out and there was

a burst of activity amongst the sound engineers and the cameramen.

'Going for a take,' called the production manager, but Kelsie had lost interest. Unobtrusively, she slipped through the crowd of sightseers and into a nearby café. It turned out to be an old-fashioned tea shop that scorned tea bags and offered home-made cakes. With slightly guilty relish Kelsie ordered a pot of tea and a cream meringue, pulling a crumpled copy of *Horse and Rider* from her shoulder-bag.

Next morning at the station, Kelsie regretted having finished the magazine. The one bookstall open on a Sunday had nothing that she wanted to read.

'Never mind.' Kelsie leaned out of the corridor window to talk to her mother. 'I expect I'll sleep most of the way back to Penloe.'

'Sorry the party went on so late, dear – Oh, the train is about to leave. Don't forget to give everyone my love, and *please* write occasionally.' Mrs Forbes walked alongside the slowly moving train.

'I'll try, Mum,' called Kelsie above the noise. 'But what with my evening sessions at the Tech. and the BHS certificate and helping Jean – '

'I know, I know . . . just try.' Mrs Forbes stood still and waved.

'Promise!' Kelsie waved back and then left the window to find the nearest seat.

Having stowed her bags, she was ready to settle down for a nap, but a young woman sitting opposite immediately began a conversation.

'That was Nurse Bella – I mean Ellen Forbes,

wasn't it? And you're her daughter? I heard you call her "Mum".'

'Yes, I am.' Kelsie did her best to sound politely off-putting, but the woman was determined to talk. She informed Kelsie that Nurse Bella was her favourite character in the show, and that in her opinion Bella was simply made to be the vicar's wife.

'I reckon they'll get married. That's what it's all been leading up to. What do you think?'

Kelsie knew she mustn't give away the plot of future episodes and tried to end the conversation, but her fellow-traveller was now appraising her closely, taking in her tousled copper curls, green eyes and freckled nose.

'You don't look a bit like her.' The woman's critical gaze went to Kelsie's scruffy bags. 'Going on holiday, then?'

'No, I'm going home.'

'Don't you live with your mother?' The voice was almost accusing. Kelsie explained how important it was for her to live at Crantock with Jean Lanyon, who was an old friend of her mother's. It had always been her dream to live in Cornwall and work with horses and now the Lanyons had made it all possible.

'And are you still at school?'

'No, I've left. I'm training to be a riding instructor. I already help the others with the stables.'

'The others?' The woman produced a bundle of complicated-looking knitting.

'Well, there's Mr Lanyon. He works at home, and has done most of the rebuilding and land clearing that was needed before the school opened last year. Jean – Mrs Lanyon – runs the school. Roger, the eldest son, is very busy with his own horses because he wants to be a breeder, but he does quite a bit of teaching. He's already got the Assistant's certificate that I'm working for, and he'll be getting the Intermediate soon. Then there's Toby. He's thirteen and a brilliant jumper and would do that all the time if he was allowed – '

Her listener interrupted.

'Didn't you ever want to be an actress, like your mother?'

'Lord, no!' Kelsie was genuinely startled by the idea. 'It would bore me to tears.' The woman stopped knitting.

'Some people would consider acting a very exciting life, and looking after animals very routine.' Kelsie thought for a moment.

'Yes, some of the work is routine. Horses need regular care and exercise. And there's so much to do that you have to have a routine to make sure it all gets done. But life at Crantock is never boring. Sometimes it's really exciting. Take last year, for instance!' Kelsie leaned forward, her eyes sparkling. The woman nodded and went on with her knitting.

Thus encouraged, Kelsie began her story. It *had* been an amazing summer, after all. It had begun with the rescue of the cart pony, Butterscotch. Then there had been their secret schemes to help Crantock's shaky finances, their outwitting of the kidnappers of their neighbour's famous stallion Chevalier d'Argent . . . and Jean and Kelsie's mother organizing things so that she could make Crantock her home. After that, they had coped with a hard autumn and winter programme of rebuilding the stables and planning for the opening of Crantock as a riding school. Having enthusiastically recounted all this to such an attentive audience Kelsie was almost sorry when she changed trains at Birmingham and left her listener behind. Crantock was worth talking about.

However, there was one confidence Kelsie had not shared, even with her mother. In fact she had mentioned it to no one. When life was looking so rosy it seemed ungrateful to have even the smallest dissatisfaction with it. Until this week away, Kelsie had been so occupied that she had not had a moment to identify the small niggling feeling under all her happiness. Now, as the train rattled out of yet another station and headed westward through rain-drenched countryside, she shaped the feeling into a definite thought. If only she had a horse of her own.

The moment she admitted it, she felt cross with herself. After all, when she'd lived in London, she had been lucky if she saw a horse from one month to the next. At Crantock she was surrounded by horses. She lived and breathed horses – eighteen of them – and now she thought about them lovingly in turn. All the old friends were still there: Alexander, the ancient hunter, Sam the carthorse, Piper and Rupert, Toby's Firecracker and Roger's Sorrel, Ladystream and her foal, Fallow. Then of course there was dear Butters, who had been her special responsibility since that fateful afternoon in the back streets of Penloe when she and Toby had rescued him from a beating. But although Kelsie was quite small, she had really got too big for Butterscotch, and anyway, he was now the sought-after favourite of the younger riders at the school.

There were nine new horses and ponies, too. Columbine, Windswept, Ranger and Dormouse had come from Trevoran Stables when they had been closed down. Jester, Baggins, Granada, Comfrey and the little Shetland, Cinders, had come from auctions or private sales, all carefully chosen by Mrs Lanyon for their good health and tempers. Kelsie loved them all in different ways, but none of them was hers and hers alone. In her free time she had the pick of them as a mount, and Rupert and Windswept in particular were a joy to ride . . . but still, there wasn't a horse at Crantock that she could point out and say 'That's mine!'

It took a couple of hours of staring at the drops of rain forming moving patterns on the carriage window for her to come to the conclusion that this was an unprofitable state of mind. As the train crawled with tantalizing slowness over the Saltash bridge into Cornwall, she excused herself with the thought that, after all, Toby had Firecracker all to himself and Roger owned Sorrel, Ladystream and Fallow. It was getting dark now, and her sandwiches and flask of coffee were long since finished. Kelsie swayed along the corridor in search of a buffet car, only to find it had been disconnected at Bristol.

Even so, she returned to her compartment feeling better. Her week in Manchester had been more fun than she had expected, even the party hadn't been too bad, and now she was nearly home. And it was spring. Soon it would be May, June and another glorious summer. And all the work to be done! The classes and rides, last year's failed O-levels to re-take, lending Roger a hand, the Pony Club, the egg round, the local horse shows. There was so much to look forward to. She began to peer into the darkness to try and catch the precious moment when the train went through the cutting and came out alongside Penloe Bay. That was the moment to pull her luggage down from the rack.

2

Pony Club

Mr Lanyon had lit a fire in the living-room at Crantock. Although the day had been spring-like, there was still a chill in the old granite farmhouse in the evenings and rain had been forecast, spreading from the north.

'I bet it rains tomorrow, Monday being our day off,' grumbled Roger, switching off the radio. As the weekend was Crantock's busiest time, Monday was officially a free day, although, as his brother Toby was fond of pointing out, *he* still had school, Kelsie had an evening class and usually had to spend the day catching up on written work, and the others always had what their mother cheerfully called 'maintenance' to do around the house, garden, fields and stables.

This Sunday had been particularly busy, as with the finer weather more and more people were ringing up to book rides and lessons. The car park that the Lanyons had reluctantly made from part of the Long Meadow had been full all day.

Only Roger, Mrs Lanyon, the cats and Kelsie's border collie, Ajax, were enjoying the fire, for Mr Lanyon had gone to meet Kelsie's train and Toby had been away all afternoon on a trip to Camborne with a friend. Suddenly Ajax pricked up his ears. He had heard a car bumping its way down the lane. At the sound of car doors slamming he sprang up.

'Calm down, Ajax. Yes, it's Kelsie at last.' Mrs Lanyon put a hand on his collar, for knowing Kelsie's habit of transporting all her belongings in numerous carrier bags she could foresee a collision in the hall. In a moment Kelsie was at the living-room door with two carrier bags in one hand, leaving the other free to fend off the loving attentions of her dog.

'He's missed me!'

'We've all missed you,' laughed Mrs Lanyon.

'And how,' added Roger feelingly. 'I've had to take out four extra rides, and mucking-out has taken ages.'

'I thought Janet Patterson was going to come to help before school.'

'She has. But she natters even more than you do, and hasn't got as much muscle power.'

'I don't believe it! A compliment at last.' Kelsie handed a bag to Mrs Lanyon and sank into a chair.

'That's for you, Jean. From Mother. We went to buy me a dress for the party and couldn't resist getting one for you as well. Go on, look. It's really nice.'

Cautiously Jean Lanyon unfolded an Indian cotton dress in soft greys, pinks and browns. She held it up for Roger's inspection.

'Hey, that's not bad, Mother. I like the belt with the little bells on.'

'I've got one, the same only different,' Kelsie explained. Roger lifted an eyebrow. 'I mean, it's the same kind of Indian design, but in a different style and colour.'

'It's lovely!' Mrs Lanyon sounded both pleased and surprised.

'I'm sure it'll suit *you*, Mum,' encouraged Roger, 'but the thought of Kelsie in any kind of dress . . . How was the party, by the way?'

'OK. Quite fun.' Kelsie settled Ajax at her feet and a cat stalked across the room to leap into her lap. 'You'd have hated it though. Not a single person there who knew a thing about horses.'

'Are you implying I'm narrow-minded?' began Roger, as his father walked in.

'You two aren't arguing already, are you?' he enquired mildly. 'Toby not back yet?'

'Not yet,' replied Mrs Lanyon. 'Hang on, there's a noise at the back door. That'll be him.'

Having a shrewd idea of the nature of her son's expedition to Camborne, she waylaid him in the kitchen just in time to stop him emptying a muddy sack on to the table.

'Oh no you don't, young man, take that out to the loft immediately.'

'Have a heart, Mum!' Toby was filthy but cheerful. 'It's raining and I've had to walk down from the road. Mick's dad wouldn't bring his car down the lane. He said it was too pot-holey.'

'Oh Lord!' Mrs Lanyon was momentarily side-tracked. 'If the lane's too rough for Mr Jenkins, then our customers will soon be complaining. We'll have to do something about it . . . *No* – I'm sorry, Toby, but I don't want all your junk in the kitchen. Put it back in the sack and leave it in the back porch. I take it you found a good dump up at Camborne?'

'Smashing, Mum. Only Mick and I and one or two

others know about it so far, so I got lots of good stuff – some bottles and a flat iron and – '

'Lovely, dear. Now clear away that sack and go and run a bath while Roger and I get supper. You can tell us all about it then.'

Supper was a hilarious meal, with Kelsie doing impersonations of the actors from 'Pringle's Parish'. Despite Ellen Forbes being in it, it was not a show that the Lanyons greatly admired. Not having a television, they had dutifully trooped round to a friend's house on a couple of occasions to watch, but even Kelsie's loyalty to her mother didn't stretch to defending the banality of the script.

Halfway through the meal, one of the cats ventured under the table, only to come nose to nose with Ajax, who took immediate exception to this invasion of his territorial rights to dropped crumbs. The ensuing scrimmage would have overturned a less sturdy table. When order was finally restored, the topic of conversation turned once more to Crantock and plans for the coming week. Mrs Lanyon brought the family diary to the table.

'Don't forget to consult the stable planner for details of the week's rides and lessons. Kelsie's doing the evening meal this week. Tomorrow there's a Pony Club meeting at five, so we'll have a late meal so that Kelsie can go. Tuesday the vet's coming for a routine check. Wednesday, egg round as usual and a nine-thirty dentist appointment for Toby . . .' (Toby pulled a mock-terrified face) 'and the farrier will be here on Thursday. Friday – nothing out of the ordinary. We'll plan for the weekend on Friday. It looks like another busy one.'

'Where's the Pony Club meeting?' Kelsie wanted to know.

'Tolwidden this month. Jane rang this morning to find out if Toby and Roger would be there. She's going to put the jumps up.'

'I suppose so.' Toby was rather offhand. 'Firecracker's getting very bored with those little jumps. We ought to make some more.'

'Well, count me out of course-building this year. I've got enough on my plate.' Roger rose from the table. There was no need to ask where he was going, for he never failed to pay a goodnight call on his precious mares and the foal.

This was the cue for clearing the table. The routine for running the household that they had decided on seemed to be working well, reflected Kelsie, as she filled a tray with dirty plates. Even Toby had come to realize that his mother couldn't possibly run the stables, do housework and provide all the meals.

After a lot of discussion it had been agreed that everyone would take care of their own bedrooms and be responsible for a particular area of the house. The living-room had fallen to Kelsie, the dining-room and stairs to Roger, and the bathroom and hall to Toby. To begin with Toby had quite approved of this arrangement. The hall had to be prevented from becoming a general dumping ground, but its stone-flagged floor didn't show the dirt too badly. He positively enjoyed sloshing around in the bathroom, polishing the brass taps and scouring the high old-fashioned bath-tub with its funny claw feet. It was a kind of poetic justice, the family considered, that

Toby, a walking magnet for dirt, should be the bathroom cleaner.

Everyone got their own breakfast and cleared it away. Everyone got their own lunch, as and when they could, and there was a rota for preparing the evening meal. Mr and Mrs Lanyon did a weekly shop in Penloe on a Monday morning when it was quiet, and Kelsie did the egg round to Methion village in the trap on Wednesdays. Meanwhile, Mr Lanyon locked himself in his study when he was working at the translations he did for an educational publisher. Otherwise he was to be found in the garden or in Crantock's steep and scrubby outlying fields, hedging and ditching or clearing gorse and bracken. On these tasks he was often joined by Roger and Kelsie, for all the new horses meant that more grazing was urgently needed, even though the Long Meadow and Five-acre were in good shape and they had successfully drained the field either side of the stream.

As she made her way to the kitchen, Kelsie put thoughts of Manchester and 'Pringle's Parish' firmly behind her. Crantock was the real world and its horses were the 'stars'. She could hardly wait for the morning so that she could be riding again.

Opening the stable planner next morning, Kelsie found that most of the riding-school horses had had a very busy week. She debated whether to tack up Alexander. He'd done some quiet hacking with Mrs Lanyon during the winter to ease his rheumaticky joints, but Kelsie rarely rode the old hunter because of his size. She hesitated and then reached for

Rupert's bridle. On the gypsy pony she would stand some chance of keeping up with Roger on Sorrel. She would take one of the others to the Pony Club meeting. Quickly she saddled Rupert and joined Roger in the yard. Sorrel was in a skittish mood, in no temper for the collected trot round the yard that her owner was determined on. She laid back her ears and danced a few crab-wise steps towards Rupert. Kelsie mounted and waited by the gate while Roger turned the mare and went on to complete the circle at a fast, but controlled, trot. He then joined Kelsie and they took the horses through the gate and into the Five-acre.

'Little madam,' muttered Roger. 'She's not had nearly enough work done on her this winter.' They discussed Sorrel's progress as they took the track that led to the stretch of wild moorland known as Methion Carn. In six weeks' time the mare was due to go to stud at Colonel Standish's. *Chevalier d'Argent* was to be the sire – part of Roger's reward for helping to foil last summer's kidnap attempt. The resulting foal would be worth a lot of money in any breeder's terms and Roger was planning happily for the future. Ladystream, too, was due to be put into foal, and, although the sire would be less distinguished than Chevalier, Roger had high hopes.

'He's the same sire as we had for Fallow and she's a little beauty, so next year Crantock will have two more handsome foals.'

Kelsie never tired of listening to Roger's plans for horse-breeding. Recently he'd seemed slightly withdrawn and taciturn, perhaps overtired by all the hard work involved in opening the school, so she was relieved to find him more like his old self. Perhaps he really had missed her, Kelsie thought, as the horses broke into a canter on the broad track that cut across the top of the carn.

It was a windy day, but the sky had been swept clear of rain and they had good views down to the sea and across to the Three Sisters mine stacks.

'Remember that time when we stopped Janet and Ranger galloping down a mine shaft?' Kelsie shivered.

'Yes.' Roger reined Sorrel in for a moment. 'That reminds me. A bit of a problem blew up with Janet while you were away.'

'Janet? A problem?' Kelsie was surprised. Janet Patterson was a lively eleven-year-old, a great ally of Toby and a dedicated admirer of Roger and Kelsie.

'Well, as you know, she spends every minute she can at the stables, and she is quite a help for her age. But she's getting very possessive about Butters.'

'She was the first person to ride him, after me,' Kelsie pointed out.

'Yes, but now Butterscotch is part of the riding school, and he's needed by other children. He's particularly good with learners, and doesn't get fed up on the lunge. Janet rides with us every day and seems to think she can always have him. Last Friday she blew up when I said she couldn't, and didn't come to Crantock all weekend.'

Kelsie sighed.

'I'd better see what I can do. Perhaps she'll turn up at Pony Club this afternoon.'

Sorrel and Rupert were beginning to fidget, so Kelsie and Roger gave them their heads. The carn was littered with stones and large boulders scoured into strange shapes by the Atlantic winds, but the track was clear and both of them knew this part of the moor like the back of their hands. Kelsie took deep gulps of salty air as the sun came out from behind the racing clouds and they galloped past the Giant's Thumb-ring, the circle of standing stones on the highest part of the carn. Sorrel gave a little leap as the track passed in their shadow and she was still excited when they reached one of the ways off the carn that the Lanyons had always called the 'Canyon'. Here the track went between two massive outcrops of rock and looked just like the proverbial pass where Indians ambush cowboys. It had been a favourite playground for the Lanyon boys and Kelsie when they were younger, and the long-suffering Piper had been trotted through the Canyon to certain death time and time again.

Now, however, Sorrel was refusing to go through it at all. The space between the rocks was quite wide and the track leading to the gate on to the road was straight ahead, but the mare jibbed and snorted and looked set to throw a tantrum. Kelsie tactfully overtook and trotted Rupert through, though she only had to wait a few seconds before Roger and his mare emerged.

'She doesn't keep it up for long these days. Just the occasional reminder that she's got spirit. I'm hoping motherhood will calm her down.' Roger closed the gate. 'You don't mind going home by road? I wouldn't mind her meeting some traffic – not that there will be much on this lane.'

Kelsie didn't mind. To be riding with Roger was a

rare pleasure these days and she was enjoying every minute of it.

Janet Patterson biked over to Tolwidden after school, having changed into her new jodhpurs in the girls' toilets.

'New jodhpurs,' she thought bitterly as she pushed her bike up a steep hill. Her mother never minded buying new clothes for her, but when it came to asking for a pony, Mrs Patterson just raised her eyes heavenwards and sighed with impatience.

'I wouldn't mind if I never had a new article of clothing ever again,' mused Janet, as she noticed a smear of oil on one leg, 'if only I could have a pony. A dun-coloured pony with black points.' Tears sprang to her eyes as she paused at the brow of the hill to catch her breath. She must hurry. If she got to the vicarage in time to offer to help, Jane might lend her Kelpie. The vicar's daughter had a Welsh Cob, well suited to her age and weight, and her own pony Kelpie was in semi-retirement. It was very likely that the good-natured Jane would offer Kelpie when she realized Janet was without a mount.

Of course, Jane being Jane, she would ask straight out why Janet hadn't come as usual with Kelsie and Toby and the other children from Methion village. She would have to think of some non-committal excuse. She skimmed down the long hill, her plaits flying out behind her, as with one hand she searched her jacket pockets for a hanky.

If Jane noticed Janet's red-rimmed eyes, she for once did not comment, and she accepted the younger girl's explanation for arriving early to help with a relieved – 'Good for you. No one else is here yet and I've not finished putting up the jumps. Tell you what, you can ride Kelpie this afternoon if Butterscotch isn't coming.' Janet's face immediately brightened, and she set to work with a will.

She was glad to be occupied when Kelsie and Toby arrived. They were early too, as Kelsie was going to instruct some of the younger riders in the next field. Jane's greeting carried clearly across the paddock.

'Hi Toby! Hi Kelsie . . . on Comfrey today, I see. Every time a different horse!' Janet didn't catch Kelsie's reply, as she straightened up from arranging some straw bales, but she winced as she heard Jane announce, 'Janet's here, helping with the jumps. I'm lending her Kelpie. What's up with Butters, then? Not lame, I hope?' Blushing, Janet bent over the bales again, as Firecracker and his rider trotted over.

'Janet Muriel Patterson!' Toby accosted her. 'Whatever are you playing at?' Janet kicked a bale into position.

'Oh shut up, Toby, I wish I'd never told you my beastly middle name.'

'I shall call you Janet Muriel in front of the entire Pony Club if you don't explain why you haven't been to Crantock. We waited ages for you.'

'I was late out of school . . . thought I'd come straight here,' mumbled Janet, refusing to meet Toby's eye as he brought the bright little chestnut up close.

'Liar!' said Toby cheerfully as he slid out of the saddle. 'You're still sulking about Butterscotch. Look, you can borrow Cracker for a bit, pop him over a few jumps if you like.'

Janet knew this was generous of Toby. Mindful of Firecracker's potential as a first class jumper and member of the Pony Club team this year, he rarely lent his pony. But she could not bring herself to be gracious.

'No, thanks,' she said stiffly, marching towards the next jump. 'I'll be getting my own pony very soon anyway, so I won't need to borrow Crantock's precious horses.' She regretted the boast the moment it was spoken, for immediately Toby was full of interest.

'Are you? That's fantastic! What breed? Where are you getting it from?'

Janet was saved from replying by a loud hail from Jane. Members were now arriving in force, and if Janet wanted to join in the instruction ride she would have to tack up Kelpie quickly. Thankfully she ran round to the vicarage utility room to collect the tack. Bumping into the vicar on the way out again gave her conscience a nasty tweak. Lying about getting her own pony could only go from bad to worse, having to talk about it, explaining why it hadn't arrived yet . . . Oh, why had she been so silly? Feverishly she caught and bridled a startled Kelpie. She had just buckled the girths of the worn saddle, when she heard the gate creak behind her. She spun round and there was Kelsie, looking delighted.

'Congratulations, Jan! Toby's just told me the good news about your pony!'

'Oh, he *would*,' wailed Janet, and promptly burst into tears.

It took a while to get things started. In general,

members seemed to prefer what Mrs Lanyon would call a 'mounted mother's meeting' to practical work. She herself had arrived late in the old Morris Traveller to find the group deep in a post-mortem on the Easter rally in Penloe, when several West Cornwall branches had met to hold competitive events. Kelsie was nowhere to be seen, and the younger children and their ponies were milling around in an aimless way in the next field. However, the paddock was all ready, with a course laid out for the more experienced jumpers, so briskly she set about sorting out the group.

Meanwhile, Kelsie had heard a full confession from Janet, not only about her fib to Toby, but also how much she wanted a pony, 'just like Butterscotch'. Kelsie found herself in complete sympathy, and had admitted in her turn how much she wanted a horse of her own. Seeing Janet's surprised face, she had pointed out that being surrounded by horses in your daily life was not the same as having one of your very own. Then Kelsie had put a friendly arm round Janet's shoulders and suggested they both put brave faces on the situation.

'Let's enjoy what we have got. Comfrey gave me a lovely ride over here. You've got dear little Kelpie for an hour or two. And you know you're welcome at Crantock any time and Jean'll let you ride Butterscotch whenever it's reasonable. Tell you what . . .' Kelsie led the way to the field. 'How about learning to drive the jingle? You could come with me and Piper on the egg round before school, if you like.'

It was a much-comforted Janet that trotted out to

meet her friends as Kelsie waved to Mrs Lanyon in the paddock and set about her instruction session.

Half an hour later, Kelsie was intrigued to notice a head-scarved figure in a tweedy suit leading a sturdy brown New Forest pony into the paddock. His rider was sitting rather oddly, a little too far forward and slightly to one side. The girl was about Toby's age and was smiling broadly as they came to a halt. She jolted in the saddle and tipped even more to one side, but the head-scarved lady put up both hands to a broad belt at the child's waist and settled her back. Jean Lanyon called to Kelsie to come over, so she told her riders to continue their figure-of-eights without her.

'Don't you forget, I've got eyes in the back of my head,' It was a passable imitation of their missing organizer, and a hoot of laughter followed Kelsie as she climbed over into the paddock.

'Come and meet Mrs Bourne-Lacey and Caroline,' called Mrs Lanyon. 'I helped them to choose Gypsy here.'

'I can't tell you what a marvellous time we've had since Gypsy arrived,' Mrs Bourne-Lacey enthused.

'I've certainly never seen Caroline smile so much.' Mrs Lanyon turned to Kelsie. 'Caroline is spastic, and doesn't have a lot of control over her arms and legs, so there are a lot of activities she can't join in. It occurred to me that a quiet, reliable pony would be just the thing for getting her out and about and giving her an interest.'

Here Caroline joined in the conversation, and although at first Kelsie had difficulty in following her speech, she gathered that Caroline wanted to join the children in the next field. Kelsie was only too pleased to help, and so Caroline and Gypsy went to follow a small rider also on a leading rein.

Looking across from the paddock, Mrs Lanyon was pleased to see that Kelsie found time to help Caroline sit more comfortably in the saddle, and that by the end of the session she was beginning to improve her balance. As riders and ponies began to leave the field, a plan began to form in her mind. She was about to call over to Kelsie, when a commotion among the jumping enthusiasts in the paddock distracted her attention.

Toby was bored. After finishing another clear round on Firecracker, he realized that his mother wasn't even watching him. She was chatting with the woman from the Manor who was said to have a peculiar daughter. That must be the one, on the nondescript brown pony. Funny, the Bourne-Laceys were fearfully well off. You'd think they would have bought something more showy.

The brown pony was led off into Kelsie's class, and his mother's attention was once more with the riders in the paddock. Toby's next round of the course received some criticism.

'Yes, Toby, I know you jumped clear – but it was no thanks to you! You paid no attention to his stride on the last three jumps.' Toby heartily wished his mother elsewhere. As he trotted Firecracker to join the others, he could see that idiot Billy Pender grinning like an ape.

The two boys were still bickering when Mrs Lanyon called it a day.

'You're getting too big for your boots, Toby Lanyon,' jeered Billy. 'If Miss Clay were here, she'd take you down a peg or two.'

'It's not my fault these pathetic little jumps are too easy for Cracker. We know the course backwards – I could do it blindfold.'

'Couldn't.'

'Could.'

'Couldn't.'

'Could! And I'll jolly well show you. Jane, lend us that scarf of yours, will you?' The youngsters took a quick look in Mrs Lanyon's direction, but she seemed engrossed by Kelsie's instruction class. Billy brought his pony alongside Toby and tied the scarf firmly round his eyes.

'No cheating!' he warned, but Toby was too occupied with calculating the distance to the first jump to reply. There was a cheer from the rest of the group as Firecracker cantered slowly towards the three old tyres suspended from a rail.

It was the cheer that caught Jean Lanyon's attention. At first she noticed nothing unusual. The first two jumps were cleared carefully and well and it was not until the chestnut made a turn to approach the wall that she noticed the yellow scarf across Toby's face.

It was a slow, steady, unspectacular round. Firecracker tapped the rail on the last fence, but it didn't fall and Toby trotted Firecracker in the direction of his friends' applause, pulling off his scarf with a flourish. He reined in abruptly as he caught sight of his mother's face.

There followed a public lecture of the kind that

usually leaves a deep impression. Billy, Jane and the other spectators also came under fire for egging Toby on, and all of them felt very uncomfortable by the time Mrs Lanyon had finished with them.

'Really, Toby,' she concluded, 'for someone who is usually so concerned for Firecracker's well-being, you've shown no sense at all this afternoon. The pony's matured more than you have in the last year. You certainly couldn't have played that trick with him last summer. Still, one useful thing came out of this silly blindfold experiment.'

'What?' muttered a subdued Toby.

'It was the best round you've done for a long time. You really were concentrating on his stride!'

Mercifully, that seemed to be the end of the affair. His mother and Kelsie were anxious to get back to Crantock by car, as Kelsie still had a meal to organize, so Janet was delighted to be asked to ride Comfrey. She was an undemanding companion, and Toby was able to give her a glowing description of his blindfold triumph (omitting his mother's disapproval) that lasted most of the way back home.

They had reached the road that led to Methion village and the Patterson's bungalow, when Janet remembered the news that she had forgotten because of her upset over Butterscotch.

'Hey, did you know the circus is in Penloe next week?'

'No. Which one is it?'

'Not one that's been before. It's called Harvey's Family Circus and there are horses all over the poster. Do you want to go?'

'If there are horses. I'll ask the others.'

Happy at the thought of an outing with her idols from Crantock, Janet dismounted and handed Comfrey's reins to Toby. She said goodbye and whistled her way cheerfully up the garden path. For a moment she pictured herself leading a pony into a loose-box at the back of the bungalow to be unsaddled, fed and watered. Then she brushed the daydream aside. If she set the alarm for six tomorrow morning, she might get to Crantock with enough time for a short ride on Butterscotch before school.

3

Harvey's Family Circus

It was a busy week for all of them at Crantock. The school was fully booked for lessons and rides and the weather was mild. Kelsie rejoiced in the banks of primroses along the winding lanes and the heady scent of the gorse up on the moor. She enjoyed helping with the classes – it was a revelation sometimes to watch Mrs Lanyon encourage a nervous rider or tactfully restrain an over-confident one – but Kelsie's first love was riding cross-country. She had to take care, though. Her priority when out with a ride was to keep an eye on 'the customers' and their mounts, and it was a temptation to get carried away by the beauty of a spring afternoon, or her current day-dream that she was riding her very own horse.

This creature of her imagination was a strange animal, capable of changing its shape and colour by the hour. One day it was a palomino gelding, the next, a grey Anglo-Arab mare. After that it might become a dark chestnut or a jet-black thoroughbred. The possibilities were endless.

One afternoon, she was so carried away by the process of turning comfortable, ordinary Jester into a pure-bred Arab of fiery temper, that she failed to notice that she had lost two of her riders at the last gate. Precious minutes were wasted going back for them.

The family saw little of Roger. He tore through the stables like a whirlwind in the early morning, mucking out, grooming and distributing feeds at a rate that left everyone else behind. Then he was off to see to his own horses, always reappearing just in time to take his lessons or rides, always finishing punctually so that he could return to his own work, which now included breaking and schooling ponies for friends. When he had his breakfast or lunch was a mystery, and many of his evening meals that week were left drying out in the Rayburn.

Toby, perhaps taking his mother's lecture to heart, threw himself into his training programme for the Pony Club team. At the same time he was very involved with his new camera, a good one that he had just bought with his savings from this winter's dumping expeditions. He had been forbidden to take the camera to school, but as soon as he came home he was to be found taking photographs from every corner of Crantock. He even rode with the camera around his neck, choosing the faithful Piper as a mount. The piebald could be relied on to behave as if reins mattered not one bit, if both rider's hands were busy adjusting the lens or rolling on film. Sadly, Toby soon ran out of film in an orgy of snapping, and his current finances would not allow him to rush into Penloe for any more.

Mrs Lanyon appeared on the surface to be her usual busy self, while Mr Lanyon's spare time was so taken up with filling in the pot-holes in the lane, that he failed to notice her preoccupied manner. If he had, he would have realized that she was 'hatching something' as the family called it. Neither did anyone notice that Mrs Lanyon spent quite some time on the telephone each evening and wrote a good many letters, but then it was a particularly hectic week.

At half-past seven on Wednesday morning, Janet arrived at Crantock to find Kelsie hastily packing eggs on the huge kitchen table.

'I've run out of egg boxes,' complained Kelsie. 'Oh good, you've brought yours back. That makes four more. Get the big basket from the still-room would you, Jan, and put four dozen for the "Rose and Crown" in it.'

They packed eggs in companionable silence. Janet loved the kitchen. Her own kitchen had what the adverts called 'a Space-Age Design' of gleaming white formica, easy-to-clean vinyl floor and split-level oven. Like Kelsie, she preferred the look of Crantock's old dresser, bulging with oddments of china, storage jars, cookery books and an assortment of items from a jar of peacock feathers to a tin of linseed oil. The only working surface, apart from the marble slab in the still-room that was used for pastry-making, was the wooden table. A couple of ancient armchairs, usually commandeered by the cats, were drawn up to the comforting warmth of the Rayburn. Mrs Patterson would have shuddered and said 'how unhygienic', but to Janet the kitchen was heaven.

It was heaven too to be harnessing Piper to the jingle amid all the cheerful morning sounds of a busy stable. Ajax decided to keep the girls company and jumped into the cart, his tongue hanging out in an expectant manner. Mr Lanyon gave them a wave as he led Windswept and Granada through the Five-acre gate. He always lent a hand on Wednesday mornings while Kelsie delivered eggs to Methion village.

First, however, they were to deliver to their neighbour, Colonel Standish, and Janet had the pleasure of taking the reins for all of the Colonel's long, smoothly tarmaced drive. Piper stepped out bravely and Janet listened carefully to Kelsie's instructions. It was another lovely morning with little traffic to spoil their enjoyment, but all too soon Kelsie looked at her watch and found it was twenty to nine.

'Only half the round done, thanks to me not getting the eggs sorted out last night. Sorry, Jan, but if I don't let you out just here you'll never catch the school bus. Don't forget your bag.'

Janet jumped down from the jingle and patted Piper, producing half a carrot from her coat pocket.

'Thanks a lot. That was lovely, Kelsie. And it's decided then? About Friday week. All of us are going?'

'All of us except Jean and Hugh. They can't stand circuses. Roger nearly refused to come because of being so busy, but as it's supposed to be Toby's birthday treat, he relented.' Janet heard the sound of the school bus labouring round the steep bends further up Pencarn hill and prepared to flag it down. The driver stopped with obvious reluctance and Janet had a ticking-off for not catching the bus at the proper pick-up point. Kelsie could see that she didn't appear to be too cast down as she struggled to a window to wave a cheery goodbye. Ajax barked a farewell and Kelsie raised her whip, allowing the bus to pass. Then she clicked her tongue at Piper. There was still half a trap full of eggs to deliver to the top end of the village and she must be on her way.

Friday the fourth of May, Toby's birthday, started well. By making a supreme effort, everyone managed a communal breakfast so that Toby could open cards and presents with the family. Only Roger was impatient to be off.

'Couldn't all this wait until supper?'

'No, it couldn't.' Mrs Lanyon pushed him back into his seat. 'You may have grown sufficiently blasé about birthdays to leave parcels unopened until the evening, but the rest of us haven't.' That had always been one of the nice things about the Lanyons, thought Kelsie, the way they enjoyed giving and receiving presents.

Mr Lanyon was frying the last panful of bacon and eggs, and as he skilfully slid them on to plates he announced, 'Right, that's mine and Jean's done. Present opening may begin, as Toby's plate seems to be empty.'

Toby was well pleased with his birthday haul. He'd already been consulted by his parents about their present, so the new hacking jacket wasn't a surprise. Toby was so delighted to have something smart to wear for shows that Mrs Lanyon was able to stifle her regrets that they could not afford a new saddle for Firecracker. Roger's present was greeted with a whoop of joy as well. It was a flash attachment for the new camera and a roll of colour film. Although

Toby's expression was a little suspicious as he felt Kelsie's parcel and realized it was a book, he was genuinely pleased to unwrap a copy of a lavishly illustrated *Collector's Bottles*.

'Thanks, Kelsie, I've been wanting this for ages.'

There remained a pile of cards and letters and Toby hastily ripped his way through them, discovering a clutch of book and record tokens from more distant relatives and friends.

'I wish the saddler's did tokens,' he sighed, and was reproved for ingratitude by his father.

The evening meal had to be early as the youngsters were all going out, so Mrs Lanyon lent Kelsie a hand to produce Toby's favourite menu of chicken with roast potatoes and all the trimmings, followed by chocolate mousse. Janet had joined them for the meal, bringing with her a long, tubular parcel. It turned out to contain a poster of Toby's favourite show jumper, with three bars of Fry's chocolate cream hidden in the middle. Toby and Janet rushed upstairs to find a space for the poster on the bedroom wall while Kelsie helped clear the table and Roger collected car keys and money from his father. Minutes later, the old Morris was making its way down Pencarn hill towards Penloe, while Mr and Mrs Lanyon surveyed the washing-up.

'Well, I hope they enjoy themselves.' Mrs Lanyon turned on the tap. 'Nothing would induce me to go to a circus any more. I do so loathe performing animals.'

Her husband took a clean tea-towel from the dresser drawer.

'I trust that there will be some horses, at any rate,

otherwise there will be four very disappointed people!'

Roger parked the car close to the show field, and they walked through an entrance that had been rigged up with bunting and a scarlet-lettered sign that read 'Welcome To Harvey's Family Circus'. The area was full of people and there were quite a number of familiar faces from Penloe and Methion including Pony Club members, lured along by the same poster that had so attracted Janet.

On the way to the box-office they passed a caravan plastered with posters, two of which caught their attention. One showed a rearing stallion of ferocious appearance, with people running in all directions from his flying hooves. The billing underneath said 'TORNADO – Wild Horse of The Prairies!' The other promised 'PRINCESS – The Pavlova of the Equine World!' and depicted a dazzling-white mare, pirouetting gracefully beneath a spotlight.

Janet's brown eyes shone.

'Do you think they'll be in the show tonight?'

Roger shrugged his shoulders.

'We'll try and get a programme.' A blonde girl in a little booth painted with imitation red and gold curtains took the money for their tickets and they went into the tent with a stream of other families. The tent and its ring were smaller than they had expected.

'It's a lot tattier than the circus that came a couple of years ago,' commented Roger. 'I bet the acts aren't much good.'

Kelsie dug him in the ribs.

'Don't be so pessimistic. It might be smashing –

it's Toby's treat, remember.' They scrambled up the portable seating blocks to the back row. Roger always refused to sit anywhere near the front since the embarrassment of once being accosted by a clown in the course of his act. A fair child in a shiny blue leotard handed them a programme and demanded twenty-five pence.

'Twenty-five pence!' grumbled Roger as the child skipped down the wooden steps. 'And you can hardly read it, either.' He held up a limp piece of pink paper covered in small, smudged print. The Crantock party began to pass the programme from one to another as the music began and a coloured spotlight played around the roof of the tent. Toby was struck by the appearance of the musicians.

'Good grief! They've got half Penloe Town Band there!'

'Well, it makes sense,' commented Kelsie. 'You couldn't expect a small circus to tour a band round with it. It's better than taped music, anyway.'

The performance began with a parade. There were clowns; a tall thin one with a lugubrious expression painted on his face ('Enough to scare a child to death,' hissed Kelsie) and two little ones, who might have been midgets but later turned out to be boys. The clowns led the procession, waving to the crowd and turning the occasional somersault. Then followed the little girl who had sold programmes leading a cream-coloured Shetland. The smaller children in the crowd went 'Aaaaaah!' and Janet wriggled on the hard bench.

'I told you there'd be horses!' Roger and Kelsie exchanged a smile.

Behind the pony walked the blonde from the box-office in a glittering leotard, high boots and a flowing purple cape. She smiled and waved and threw kisses while a bearded man at her side, dressed in a corsair's costume, waved a scimitar in a threatening manner above his head.

'I wonder what their act is?' murmured Toby.

Next came an older woman, also blonde ('Mum Harvey, I bet,' guessed Kelsie) with a chimpanzee clinging to her waist. There were more 'aaaaahs' from the audience. The chimp was clad in red shorts, blue shirt and a Noddy hat complete with bell. Every now and then it drew back its lips and chattered at someone in the front row. They were followed by yet another blonde lady ('Auntie Harvey – or Granny Harvey?' wondered Toby) with some yapping poodles, and a man on a unicycle.

Last of all the curtains parted to reveal a horse and rider. It was the 'Princess' of the poster, every inch the showy creature that the artist had depicted. She was ridden by an equally elegant girl whose long, dark hair was drawn back under a silver topper. Her beautifully cut jacket was silver too, as were her high boots, and the effect was dazzling. Cleverly, she allowed the mare to dance a few steps on the spot until the performers in front of them had completed their circuit and were making their exit. Then, with infinite correctness and grace, the grey performed a collected trot of such amazing elevation that the onlookers felt as though they were watching a slow-motion film. Spontaneous applause broke out and Kelsie turned to Roger.

'A "*passage*",' she breathed. 'I never expected anything like this!'

Roger's eyes never left the ring.

'She's an Andalusian. I wonder who bred her?' Horse and rider disappeared behind the curtained exit. 'That's one act to look forward to.'

The show was much better than they had expected, and by the time the interval came they were all feeling pleased that they had come. The clowns had been rather a bore, but the unicyclist had been very entertaining, with a succession of bikes each taller than the one before. The performing poodles were not quite Roger's cup of tea. 'Bring on the tigers!' he had called out during one silly trick involving a dog dressed in a nightie pushing a pram. The rest of the party dissolved into giggles, but there was so much noise from the chattering children around them that it went unnoticed.

The two small clowns returned to do some stilt-walking, which was impressive to begin with but went on too long, and the first half closed with an act from the box-office girl, who shinned up a rope and did dangerous things at the top of it. First she performed some complicated gymnastics, and then she proceeded to fit an attachment to the top of the rope which she gripped with her teeth. The piratical-looking man held the bottom of the rope while she spun round like a helicopter blade. Janet couldn't bear to watch and said that it made her teeth ache.

However she soon had her teeth sunk into a toffee apple, bought for her by Toby from the little programme girl. The Crantock party spent the interval speculating about the Harvey family.

'Do you think they're all related?' asked Toby.

'Could be.' Roger glanced at the programme. 'You can't tell from the fancy names they use. I rather like the way they all do everything – selling tickets and programmes and then performing and assisting with each other's acts. I suppose they all have to look after the animals, take the tents down, drive the vans and that sort of thing.'

'Rather like us at Crantock,' pointed out Kelsie. 'Cleaning the house, running the stables, taking classes – then presenting ourselves at shows and gymkhanas!'

The first routine in the second half was a contrast to what had gone before. It was a knife-throwing act, billed as 'The Great Kalmari and Kara'. The swarthy corsair was the knife-thrower and the box-office girl (in a different costume) was the victim. She stood against the target board with a brave smile that soon became a little set; for the corsair's knives refused to stick in the board. They merely bounced and landed in a clattering heap at the girl's feet. The corsair muttered inaudibly and broke out into a sweat. He passed a hand over his eyes and took careful aim with his last knife.

'He reminds me of Bluto in "Popeye",' whispered Kelsie and she and the two younger ones tried to stifle their giggles. As is often the way when things go wrong, the attention of the crowd was riveted on the unfortunate knife-thrower. Not a child coughed, not a sweet-paper rustled. Then the knife flew through the air, struck close to the blonde girl's hip, and stayed there, quivering. There was relieved applause and the corsair made a desultory bow. His victim, smile restored, made to step forward. She couldn't. Still smiling bravely, she put both hands behind her on the board and pushed. With a little jerk she broke away – leaving a frill of her costume skewered to the target.

'The Great Kalmari is definitely the best act so far,' gasped Toby, with tears running down his face. But the best was yet to come. The couple reached the exit as the applause faded, but the curtain failed to swish across in its usual manner and all were able to witness the mighty slap across the face received by the despondent pirate from his irate assistant.

'What's next?' demanded a pink-faced, hiccuping Janet. Kelsie consulted the programme.

'Golly!' she exclaimed, and read out in dramatic tones, 'Tornado, the Apache stallion. A wild untameable Fury on Four Legs!'

Just then a burly figure in a cowboy suit with a microphone in his hand came into the ring, while the band played a few bars of 'The Big Country'. He held up his hand for silence.

'Ladies and gentlemen, boys and girls . . .' His voice was hushed and faintly ominous. 'Harvey's Circus are about to present to you an unrideable, untameable pinto stallion all the way from the vast prairies of America.' There was a roll of drums and the youngsters sat forward on their seats. A squealing neigh came from behind the curtain and Janet held her breath as the announcer continued, 'Ladies and gentlemen, we give you Tornado! The Terror of Texas!'

4

The Fury on Four Legs

Into the ring cantered the ugliest horse Kelsie had ever seen. He was a big raw-boned skewbald, goose-rumped and cow-hocked. There was nothing that could be said in favour of his appearance. His head was too large and his eyes too small. His gait was awkward and he tossed his head all the time as he completed a lap of the ring.

'Pinto stallion, my foot!' Toby was disgusted. 'It's a common old skewbald gelding, and an evil looking brute at that.' The music stopped with a crash of the drums as the skewbald came to a halt in the centre of the ring with a spectacular rear and a neigh that echoed round the tent.

'What is he going to do?' wondered Janet.

As if in answer, the cowboy with the microphone came forward and issued a challenge to all comers. Harvey's Circus were offering ten pounds to anyone in the audience who could stay on Tornado for more than one minute. Everyone looked at Tornado, now equipped with a western saddle, as he stood swishing his tail in the glare of the spotlight.

Toby was on his feet.

'I'll have a go!' he called above the excited chatter

of the crowd. He was pulled back into his seat by his brother's strong hand.

'Oh no you don't, you little idiot. Outfits like this don't hand round ten pound notes like peanuts, you know, and I'm not taking you home in pieces. Nice end to a birthday that would be.'

'Why don't you try, Rodge?' pleaded Janet. 'You can ride anything,' she added with flattering confidence.

'No, thank you,' her hero growled. 'I'm not prepared to make a fool of myself in public, even if others are.' For a leather-jacketed youth had just leaped into the ring and was approaching the cowboy. The burly man had meanwhile been urging someone to come forward and try their luck at the same time as warning possible contenders that any attempt would be 'entirely at their own risk.' He clapped the young man on the shoulder and produced a piece of paper on a clip-board that the youth appeared to sign with a flourish. Kelsie nudged Roger.

'A sort of disclaimer, in case things go wrong?'

'I expect so. Hang on, isn't that one of the boys – ' But the music had begun again, as an attendant held the horse by the bridle and another made to help the contestant into the saddle. A large clock face had been set up at the ring entrance, and the poodle lady was waiting in an exaggerated pose to set the second hand going.

'Go!' roared the cowboy into the microphone and the crowd screamed encouragement as the skewbald leaped, bucked and reared his way round the ring while the two attendants prudently made a dash for safety.

It was a mere seven seconds before the lad was unseated.

'It's a long way to fall,' commented Roger, as the would-be bronco buster flew through the air. He noticed that the lad landed neatly on his feet before rolling on the ground, getting up and dusting himself down. Already another contender was being 'signed-in' as Tornado came to a halt in the centre of the spotlight. If a horse could be said to grin, he was grinning, thought Kelsie.

The next contender was a middle-aged man in a suit, and a buzz of surprise went round the tent. He lasted no longer than the lad, but also had a safe landing, waving cheerfully to the crowd as he left the ring. Roger leaned towards the others.

'It's all a fix,' he said quietly. 'The first lad was waiting up at the back, and anyway, he was one of the boys who helped to bring the poodles on. And the man in the suit is part of the circus too – he was counting money in the box-office.'

'What a swiz!' complained Toby, but Kelsie gripped Roger's arm.

'Look who's in the ring now, then! *She's* not part of the Harvey family!'

It was Jane. With her customary breezy determination, she had made her way into the ring, despite the cowboy's attempts to ignore her. He decided to make the best of a bad job. He put an arm round Jane and said into the mike,

'Well now, folks, here's a brave little lady who wants to chance her luck with Tornado, is that right?' Jane's loud 'Yes, please!' made the mike boom and whistle.

'Now, I can tell you are a rider . . .' went on the cowboy.

'Well, she *is* wearing jods,' muttered Toby, impatiently.

'. . . so here's hoping you'll be a winner. Ten pounds remember, if you stay on for sixty seconds.'

'They've brought her a hard hat, and she's signing that paper,' commented Kelsie. 'Gosh, Jane has got a nerve.'

'She's got a bad attack of lunacy,' corrected Roger, witheringly. 'They may have fixed the competitors so far, but that horse is a genuine menace.'

Indeed, his next acrobatic display was very impressive. He reared and seemed to hop forward at the same time, he bucked three times in succession with a nasty twist between each buck. Then he made a vertical leap as if he were on a trampoline. Finally he very nearly stood on his ugly head before tearing round the ring, bucking as he went. Meanwhile, Jane, who had lost her stirrups at the first buck, the reins at the second and the saddle at the third, was lying on her back in the sawdust. Janet clutched Kelsie's hand in a moment of fear, but already their friend was scrambling to her feet and, red-faced, was making her way back to her seat.

'She was lucky,' said Roger, shortly, as the lights dimmed except for a spotlight on Tornado, who was continuing his cavorting around the ring as the band began to play Red-Indian style music. Once more without a saddle and in the romantic glare of the spotlight, perhaps for one moment the big skewbald looked something like a wild pinto. The music swelled, and into the ring ran a girl dressed as an

Indian squaw, a long black mane of hair streaming out from a beaded head-dress. She ran alongside Tornado for a few moments, then with a flying leap she had grasped his mane and thrown herself on his back.

The whole audience drew in its breath, as a drum rolled and Tornado reared, holding his upright position with his forefeet thrashing. Then he crashed down, the Indian girl still on his back. Amid tumultuous applause she rode him twice round the ring before making a triumphant exit.

'That was the same girl that was riding Princess!' Janet jumped to her feet, clapping furiously. 'What a rider!'

The next turns were lost on the Crantock youngsters as they chewed over what they had just seen. After all, what was a chimpanzee's tea-party, a counting Shetland and a juggler compared with the terrible Tornado?

They had calmed down by the time the entire Harvey family, excluding the raven-haired squaw, came on to perform a slick and complicated acrobatic routine. As one man, they were waiting for the last item on the programme, 'Princess – the Pavlova of the Equine World'.

They were not disappointed. The mare's rider, once more in her black and silver outfit, was cool and composed, looking as if she had never run after a wild pinto in her life. Princess's routine was an entertaining mix of High School and circus razzmatazz, and even the critical Roger could find no fault with it. At the end they clapped until their hands were sore and drummed their feet on the wooden flooring.

As soon as the finale was over, they rushed through the exit. It was getting dark, but they were all in agreement with Janet that the thing to do now was to 'go and find the horses'. Toby ran off to the car and came back with his camera.

'I'd like a photo of Princess and Tornado – Beauty and The Beast.'

They glimpsed Princess being led around one of the generator vans and followed. They caught up with the mare as she was being tied to a rough and ready hitching rail alongside Tornado and the Shetland. Roger nudged Kelsie, for the Shetland was being groomed by the lad who had been first to try for Tornado's ten pounds.

The black-haired girl was already starting work on the sweating Princess as Toby boldly went up to her.

'Is it all right if I take some photos of the horses?'

'Sure, go ahead,' she said, ducking under Princess's chin to get to the other side. Kelsie sighed with envy. The mare was as beautiful close to as she had been in the ring.

'Will they mind the flash?' Toby wanted to know.

The girl laughed.

'You could let off fireworks under their tails if you liked. It wouldn't bother them.'

'But Tornado . . . ?'

'Sure, Murphy rears and bucks in the ring, but that's what he's been trained to do. He doesn't act that way because he's highly strung.' Kelsie glanced at the skewbald. He was looking his most unprepossessing, his head down and his eyes half-closed.

Toby took several shots of all three horses, but mostly of Princess, who, as Roger had thought, was an Andalusian, bred in Spain. Her rider seemed happy to talk about the horses as she worked. Princess was being given a thorough going-over before being bedded down in the large horse-box behind them.

The girl's name was Tara, and it appeared she was a niece of the Mr Harvey who owned the circus. He was the cowboy who ran the Tornado act, and Tara's father was the Great Kalmari.

'Why did you call the skewbald Murphy, just then?' Janet asked her.

'That's his real name. He comes from Ireland – he's only five, and we haven't had him long.' She paused with the body brush in her hand, looking at him with disfavour. 'He's not an easy horse to give your heart to. He's plug-ugly for a start and eats like an elephant. Princess now . . .' Tara became lyrical about Princess, and Kelsie couldn't blame her. She rubbed the mare's nose with longing, and received a melting look from her long-lashed eyes.

'So you can see,' concluded Tara, giving the mare a final stroke with a stable rubber, 'why she's far too good for a scrubbly little outfit like this!'

Kelsie felt surprised at the disdain in Tara's voice, though of course she was quite right. Her act could be top of the bill in any big circus.

'I want to concentrate on Princess – get her into one of the top European shows. The wild horse act is rubbish, and as soon as I can get out of this dump, I will.'

'Oh, you will, will you, Tara?' came a voice from behind them, and they all swung round as the bearded knife-thrower walked towards them. The lad grooming the Shetland immediately downed tools and melted into the shadows.

'Oh, Dad!' Tara sighed in a hopeless kind of way, and as the man pushed his way past Kelsie to face his daughter, she was aware of a strong aroma of whisky.

'I trust madam is going to inform her family before she ups and leaves us in the lurch,' said the Great Kalmari bitterly, swaying on his feet.

'Look, Dad, you've known for ages that I want to get out. Let's not have a row about it now – I want to get the horses settled.' Her father protested as Tara began to lead Princess towards the box, but she cut him short with 'Leave it alone, will you. You've been drinking all evening and Auntie Vera's as mad as a hornet with you for messing up your act. No wonder she belted you one.' Tara disappeared into the van with the horse, her father following with his voice raised in protest.

'This is where we beat a retreat.' Roger began to walk away. 'Quick, before they come out again.'

As they left the show field Kelsie smiled to herself. How Rodge hated rows – even other people's. But it was time to be getting home anyway. They would be expected back at Crantock, and they had to run Janet home first.

They trooped into the kitchen to find that Mrs Lanyon had spent the evening baking. They sat down to the luxury of coffee with fruit cake.

'Make the most of it.' Mrs Lanyon bent to take a batch of biscuits out of the oven. 'It's not often I get the chance to bake these days.'

Mr Lanyon, who had been working on some

accounts at the other end of the table, asked, 'What was the circus like? Any good?' but got no distinct reply until the fruit cake was nearly demolished.

'Now what on earth made me think the cake would last for tomorrow as well?' demanded Mrs Lanyon, sinking into a chair by the Rayburn. Her question went unanswered amid a babble of voices describing Harvey's Family Circus.

When every act had been described down to the last detail, Mr Lanyon said,

'I'm glad you all had a good evening. Look, I know it's quite late, but do you mind if we round off Toby's birthday by telling you about a new scheme your mother's dreamed up for Crantock?'

'I thought something was in the air.' Roger was amused. 'What have you been up to, Mother?'

'Well,' began Mrs Lanyon, 'you remember Mrs Bourne-Lacey's daughter, Caroline, Roger? Kelsie met her last week at Pony Club, on a pony I helped choose. It was obvious how much pleasure the child was getting from riding, and that set me thinking. The Bourne-Laceys are well-to-do and can easily afford to buy and keep a pony, but there must be a lot of handicapped people in an area like West Penwith who would benefit from riding like Caroline, but who couldn't possibly have their own pony. Ordinary riding schools might not be able to cope with disabled riders . . .' she took a look round at their faces, 'but Crantock isn't an ordinary riding school, is it?'

'What are you thinking of doing?' prompted Roger.

'You've all heard of the RDA – Riding for the

Disabled Association,' Jean Lanyon went on, more briskly. 'I propose that we set up a branch here at Crantock.'

Immediately Kelsie and Roger broke in with eager questions until Mrs Lanyon had to say, 'I'm afraid I haven't worked out all the details yet. I've been gathering as much information as I could and thinking about organization and so on. There's a lot more I want to find out from the RDA and local groups that deal with the handicapped. I wanted to sound you out first, because it will mean more work for all of us, even though a lot of help will come from volunteers.' She looked round the room again. 'What do you think?'

'It's a good idea, Mum.' Roger spoke firmly. 'And I'll help all I can.' Knowing how precious time was to Roger, Kelsie felt like hugging him, but restrained herself and instead put an arm round Mrs Lanyon.

'Me too. I think it'll be a smashing thing for Crantock.'

Everyone took Mr Lanyon's support for granted – he'd clearly been included in his wife's early ideas, but it was suddenly noticed that there had not been a sound from Toby. His arms were on the table and his head was down on his arms.

'Toby! Wake up!' ordered Kelsie. Toby sat up, his face red and his brown hair ruffled.

'I wasn't asleep, I heard every word – and I think you're all round the bend!'

'Toby!' Kelsie was horrified, but he was not to be stopped.

'Completely bananas. You're always saying there aren't enough hours in the day as it is – so when is all this RDA stuff going to be fitted in? We never do anything as a family any more, because someone always has something more important to do. Six days a week we have cars belting down the lane loaded with kids. I suppose this is where our so-called day off goes west?' Both Roger and Kelsie tried to interrupt, but Toby was in full flow. 'I wish we could go back to the way we were before the riding school. We didn't have much money but we had a lot more fun – and I hate that rotten old rota!'

Toby ran from the kitchen, slamming the door behind him. For a moment the others sat in silence as his feet thudded on the old wooden staircase.

'Oh dear!' Mrs Lanyon turned to look at her husband. 'What on earth has brought all that on?'

'Over-tiredness and over-excitement I expect, dear.' He calmly filled his pipe.

'I think there's more to it than that,' said Mrs Lanyon in a troubled voice as she followed her younger son out of the room.

At ten past two on a pouring wet Saturday afternoon, Kelsie found herself on the bus from Methion with time to think about the events of the previous day. The two o'clock ride had been cancelled by a group of fair-weather riders, leaving Kelsie with just enough time to dash into Penloe to buy a pair of jeans and some new wellingtons. There was no bus back, but she had arranged a lift with a friend who was coming up for a ride at four-thirty.

Toby's got it all wrong, Kelsie thought to herself. We do get some time off, and we do do things all together, sometimes. The work is hard, but it's fun too, and if Jean reckons we can take on Riding for the Disabled as well – then we jolly well can!

She swung herself off the bus at the Market Street stop and turned down the nearest steep alley that ran down to the harbour. The rain fell heavily, in big drops, while the gutters were two streams flowing noisily seawards. Kelsie made for one of her favourite shops, the Quayside Chandlery.

She spent a satisfactory half-hour trying on jeans and browsing wistfully through a selection of expensive wet-weather clothing, none of which was suitable for riding in. She'd yet to find something that was waterproof, lightweight and which didn't get in the way.

As she selected a pair of thick-soled wellingtons she noticed a girl with a mane of dripping black hair trying on a yellow mac. It was Tara. Kelsie could not resist introducing herself, and Tara seemed pleased to see her.

'I'm glad I bumped into you,' the circus girl said as she paid at the till. 'I was sorry you found yourself in the middle of a family row last night, and I never said goodbye. How about going somewhere for a coffee and a chat?' Kelsie was only too delighted, and they dodged their way through the puddles to her old haunt, the Crow's Nest at the station end of the harbour.

They sat at an upstairs window overlooking the yachts and dinghies dipping and rising in the choppy grey water, and exchanged potted biographies over cups of weak coffee. Kelsie wanted to know how many of the performers she had seen the night before were members of the Harvey family.

'All of us, more or less,' Tara told her. 'My mother is Pa Harvey's sister.'

'Which act was your mother?'

Tara hesitated a moment.

'She's not with us any more. She's a trapeze artiste and she went off to America three years ago with her partner in the act. That's one of the reasons Dad gets so upset when I talk about leaving.' Tara's long brown fingers tore at a paper napkin. 'I have to leave. I have to. Princess could be an international star. She's special, she's got what it takes – and I have too. That's not boasting.' She looked at Kelsie pleadingly. 'It's just something I feel in my bones.'

'I understand,' sympathized Kelsie. 'It's not something I have myself, but I know that's how Toby feels about Firecracker and jumping. It seems as though he's going through a selfish phase at the moment, but it's only that he thinks that the school and Riding for the Disabled will get in the way of what he wants to do.'

'Anyway, that's enough about me,' Tara said carelessly. 'It's your turn. Tell me all about this Crantock place.'

Kelsie obliged, though it occurred to her that Tara might think her life dull, compared to her own, but she seemed interested, particularly by tales of the 'rescued' horses.

'So you take care of them, and rehabilitate them?'

'Those that are young enough. Alexander and Sam are retired – well, Alex occasionally gets ridden and Sam pulls a cart once in a while. But Toby's precious Firecracker was a rescued horse, and so is Roger's Sorrel. Butterscotch and Rupert have become very amenable school ponies.'

'That's wonderful!' Tara was full of admiration, but Kelsie wanted to know more about Princess, so the conversation returned once more to the circus.

'Dad doesn't know,' confided Tara, 'but when we have a week in Plymouth next month, a representative of the best circus in Switzerland is coming specially to see my act. The Swiss love High School acts.'

'If you leave, will the Harveys lose the wild horse act as well?'

'A good thing if they do.' Tara was contemptuous. 'It's a stupid act. That mad horse will hurt someone one day, and then the family will be in a bad mess – bad publicity, trouble with the insurance.'

Suddenly Kelsie noticed the time on the café's clock. Five past four.

'Help! I'm late for my lift. I should have been waiting outside the station at four. It was lovely meeting you again – and the best of luck!' Tara reminded Kelsie about her parcels and the two girls said a hasty goodbye. As she sprinted along the wet pavement, Kelsie thought of Tara's exciting future, travelling from one European capital to another.

She was still thinking about Tara and her beautiful mare while she was dealing with wet tack after the four-thirty ride. Her reverie was broken by Mrs Lanyon coming into the tack-room.

'Kelsie,' she said, sitting beside her and unbuckling a bridle, 'how would you like another short break from Crantock? I'm thinking of taking a little trip.'

5

Two Days Away

Ever since it had been decided to go ahead with the Riding for the Disabled scheme, Jean Lanyon's spare time had been completely taken up with letters, visits and telephone calls. She had contacted Greenhallow, the special school in Penloe, parents of handicapped children that she already knew, a physiotherapist at the local hospital and the nearest branch of the RDA at Falmouth.

A handbook and pamphlets had arrived from the organization's headquarters and they had been eagerly read by them all – except Toby, who was still refusing to take part in any discussion of the subject.

Mrs Lanyon, Roger and Kelsie visited the Falmouth branch one afternoon and came back fired with enthusiasm. Kelsie was now looking forward keenly to the two-day course for RDA instructors planned for the first week in June. She and Mrs Lanyon were to drive up to a riding centre on the north-east edge of Dartmoor.

'We're lucky to get places at such short notice,' Mrs Lanyon pointed out, 'but when I explained how anxious we were to get our scheme started this summer, they squeezed us in. Knowle is a very special place – it's very beautiful, and besides having a branch of the RDA they train handicapped school-leavers for work with horses. I think we're going to find our two days there quite an eye-opener.'

A few days before they were due to leave, a timetable arrived through the post together with instructions for finding the centre.

'Day one,' Kelsie read aloud at the breakfast table to Roger, who had just dashed in for coffee and toast, 'Nine to nine-thirty – Introduction. Ten o'clock, "The Ideal Riding Position", demonstration with commentary, followed by an analysis of a typical RDA class. Eleven-thirty, discussion followed by another lecture, "Instructors and Helpers, their aims and functions." One o'clock, lunch – golly, we'll need it by then!'

'What happens in the afternoon?'

'Let's see . . . there's a demonstration called "The lesser handicapped – how horses help" with the residential students. Then an illustrated lecture with a physio. Then tea, then another lecture on the more advanced work, then something they call "socializing" until supper.'

Roger reached for more toast.

'They certainly pack a lot in.'

'The second day sounds more active. We start in the morning with a practical class, taking turns to be instructors and pupils. That's so we know what it's like to be on the receiving end, I suppose. Then there's a talk on practical problems, special tack and equipment. After lunch – oh lor', this sounds ominous – "Mounted Instruction, Fun and Games".'

'Adapted gymkhana games, I expect, like they were doing at Falmouth. Does that take all afternoon?'

'Yes. We finish with tea and a question and answer session. Then the long drive home. We're going to be exhausted!'

'Well, you've got to be home ready for Tuesday morning,' Roger told his mother as she came into the kitchen. 'We can't possibly manage any longer without you both.'

'You'll cope very well.' Mrs Lanyon was firm. 'Sunday will be busy, but I've organized lots of help with the classes. And you've all been invited to the Pattersons for an evening meal, so I refuse to shed too many tears for my poor, neglected menfolk.'

All the same, Mrs Lanyon had a momentary twinge when on Saturday afternoon she drove the car up the lane, Kelsie at her side and two battered suitcases on the back seat.

(For once, Kelsie had dispensed with carrier bags. 'We shall be sleeping in a dormitory of some kind, and it will be much easier to keep all your things together in one case,' Mrs Lanyon had advised her.)

Kelsie shut the last gate and they headed for Penloe and the A30.

'I'm pretty certain I've thought of everything,' said Mrs Lanyon, half to herself. 'I've left copious notes on the stable planner about tomorrow.' Once they had left the town and the Morris was steadily eating up the miles at a pace suitable to its advanced years, their thoughts wandered to other things. Kelsie was pleased to have an opportunity to be alone with Mrs Lanyon for a few hours. The last month had been so hectic that there hadn't been much time to talk.

First, they discussed Toby and his attitude towards the RDA plans. His mother was fairly sure that she knew what was wrong. He was afraid of handicaps.

'Like a lot of people, he's rarely come into contact with the disabled – and we're often afraid of what we don't know. I worked in a hospital for a bit when I was young, so I learnt early on how to cope. You and Roger seem to grasp quite naturally that the handicapped have the same needs and responses as the rest of us. But Toby . . .' She sighed and glanced at the next road sign coming rapidly into view. 'Another thing that worries him,' she continued, 'is that Crantock is losing its romance.'

'Romance?' Kelsie was startled.

'Well, yes. Crantock used to be all about rescuing horses from the deadly peril, as far as he's concerned. Now that we're running the school, we just don't have the time, energy or even the room for any more crocks. Toby knows that, and I suppose taking on the RDA seems like the last straw. Oh, that reminds me of something I've been meaning to talk to you about for ages . . .' Mrs Lanyon gave Kelsie a quick look. 'I know I've just said that we're short of space, but I reckon we could manage to squeeze in one more horse. You must have thought about having your own horse at some time, Kelsie?'

For a moment Kelsie was taken aback. Had her preoccupation over the last few weeks been so obvious? Then she admitted that of course she had, that she had been saving as hard as she could, but still had a very long way to go.

'Your mother would like to help with finances, you

know. She said as much in her last letter,' put in Mrs Lanyon. Kelsie felt a sudden warm surge of joy. It *was* possible. The dream could become a reality. Jean thought it a reasonable idea, her mother too.

'All I ask is that you stick to *one* horse! Roger's animals are multiplying at such a rate that he'll soon have to start thinking about renting land. Now that we've reclaimed Crantock's neglected fields, we've reached our capacity.'

The rest of the journey, through Cornwall and over the border into Devon by way of Launceston, was taken up with a lively conversation about Kelsie's choice of horse and the general future of Crantock.

'My dream now is an indoor school,' confessed Mrs Lanyon. 'No more cancelled lessons – and what a help it would be to the RDA work.'

The sun was setting as they skirted the northern edge of Dartmoor, and Kelsie was impressed by the dark, looming tors and rugged landscape.

'It's a bit like the Carn, only on a much grander scale. It seems to go on forever – and how lovely to see the ponies in their natural surroundings!' To Kelsie, Devon had always been the county you went through in order to reach her beloved Cornwall. The red cliffs and rolling fields of South Devon were familiar to her from the train journey, but she had never been to this part of the county before.

The car left Okehampton, and the road began to bear slightly south as darkness fell. Kelsie retrieved the directions from her bag.

'We take a right-hand fork soon, and four miles further on we must look out for a signpost to the left that says "Knowle and Northteignton".'

Mrs Lanyon nodded.

'It's a pity we aren't arriving in daylight. Knowle has the most glorious position on a cliff-like hill looking back towards the moor. Oh, and I forgot to tell you, it's not a house, Kelsie. It's a castle. The last castle ever built in England!'

The Hartons of Knowle were not an old aristocratic family – 'Biscuit Barons' they had been nicknamed when the first Lord Harton had gained his title in Victoria's reign. He was a 'local boy made good' and his grocery empire had grown so large and profitable that at the turn of the century he had bought a magnificent stretch of high woodland overlooking the Teign river on one side and the edge of the moor on the other. He had then engaged the most famous architect of the day and had commanded him to build a castle – a small one, with every modern convenience.

That was one of the most disconcerting things about the place, Kelsie decided as they were being shown round the castle by the present Lady Harton after supper. There were stone corridors, panelled wood in all the rooms, leaded windows, archways and spiral staircases, and yet the finishing touches to the building, which hadn't been completed until the mid-twenties, included central heating, an internal telephone system and lifts to the upper stories. All the rooms were comfortably furnished in a late Edwardian style, and Lady Harton, her white hair drawn into a knot and wearing a long skirt, was a welcoming part of the general atmosphere.

'I know you'll all be very busy in the next few days,

in the capable hands of Avril Collier, your course leader, but do take any opportunity you can to enjoy the castle grounds. My late father-in-law made some beautiful paths through the woods and into the Teign Gorge.'

With murmurs of thanks, the group left the castle by its massive front door and made their way across the courtyard to the stable block adjoining a paddock and an indoor school. Dormitories and a dining-area had been converted from a carriage house and garages.

Kelsie caught up with Mrs Collier as they crossed the yard.

'Are Lord and Lady Harton very horsey people? Is that why the riding centre is here?'

'Lord Harton used to be a great hunting man, but neither of them keeps horses any more. They set up the stables as a charitable trust to be used as a training centre for disabled school-leavers and as a branch of the RDA. I run the place for them, but they have a great interest in all that goes on, own most of the RDA ponies, and love opening their home to all the students that come here.'

They had arrived at the dining-room, where a group of people were making coffee. Avril Collier excused herself to Kelsie.

'I must introduce myself to some of the late-comers. I like to have names attached to all the faces before we start the first session.'

Avril Collier had certainly succeeded in putting names to faces by the time they all met in the lecture-room at nine-thirty next morning and all the students had taken a liking to her. She was a short, stocky woman with greying hair and bright blue eyes, full of energy and enthusiasm. In her introduction she apologized for going over ground that might already be familiar.

'Half of you on this course have had experience as instructors or helpers, and the other half, although very experienced with horses, have not worked with the handicapped before.'

Kelsie took a quick glance round the room. There were twelve of them – ten women of all ages and two slightly self-conscious looking males, one a boy of about Roger's age and the other a military man with a luxuriant moustache. They were among the 'novice' group. The six women who were already RDA instructors had tended to stick together last night, swapping experiences from their respective groups. Kelsie was glad that she was not alone, for she was slightly apprehensive of what might be in store.

She need not have worried. The morning passed very quickly and Kelsie and Mrs Lanyon found themselves totally absorbed. The handicapped teenagers who took part in the first demonstration were very impressive and at lunch-time Kelsie was able to talk to some of them about their two-year training at Knowle. It was useful to gather some of their ideas and opinions, although these youngsters had been described to them as 'the lesser handicapped' and most of the children and adults who would eventually come to Crantock would have more severe disabilities. Jean Lanyon spent much of her lunch-time with a fork in her left hand and a ball-point pen in the right.

'I must take a few notes while I remember – I'm hopeless at writing while someone is talking. I thought what that chap said in the last lecture, about organizing volunteers and keeping them happy, was very important. We are obviously going to have to become paragons of tact and discretion, Kelsie.'

'Better keep Rodge away from the volunteers, then,' laughed Kelsie.

Like the morning session, the afternoon was equally divided between the lecture room, the paddock and the indoor school. Mrs Lanyon was very envious of the latter.

'Though we could never have a building anything like this!' For the original architect had built it in the same grand style as the castle itself.

The item on the course programme describing itself as 'socializing until supper' was interpreted by Kelsie and three of the younger set as a chance for a walk around the grounds. First they made a circuit of the craggy bluff on which the castle had been built.

'What a view!' exclaimed Kelsie as she gazed over the valley to the impressive sweep of Dartmoor. 'And what a building!' They turned to look up at the sheer granite walls of the castle. The architect had not been tempted to create Gothic turrets or fussy detail unsuitable to the surroundings, and the building rose clean and uncluttered from its setting. Behind the castle was the sheltered, level area that contained the stables, paddock and ornamental gardens. Beyond, less formal gardens swept up again into woodland.

They returned warm but hungry from their walk, with just enough time to change their clothes before supper. Tonight they were to have a meal in the castle at the invitation of Lord and Lady Harton. To everyone's relief this was an informal affair. Kelsie and her companions arrived to find the older ones already sipping sherry in the elegant drawing-room, but they were soon ushered, not to the rich and sombre dining-room they had been shown the night before, but to the original kitchens. Here they sat down at a long table and were served with homely steak-and-kidney pie followed by fruit salad. After coffee had been served, Lady Harton said with a twinkle in her eye.

'I don't suppose you young people are ready for a chat by the fireside just yet. Why don't you go for an evening ride? You must have had enough of standing about watching others all day. Avril will tell you which ponies you can take.'

Avril was only too willing.

'They haven't had a very exacting day, confined to the paddock and the school. Just make sure you get back before dark and turn them out in the field by the lodge cottage when you've done.'

They had a splendid ride. Although Kelsie would have liked to have seen the river they could hear rushing noisily through the rocky valley below, they kept to the bracken-fringed hill paths to catch the last of the evening sunshine. The ponies were fresh and eager, and returning by a woodland track they gave them their heads, reaching the castle grounds just as the sun sank behind the western edge of the moor.

By the time they had seen to the ponies and returned the tack it was nearly dark, but no one was ready for bed. Somehow there was a lot to talk about, and it was several cups of coffee later that Kelsie and the other girls were creeping into their dormitories. Kelsie glanced at the luminous hands of her watch. It couldn't be that late! And tomorrow – or rather, today – was the practical part of the course. She could only hope it wouldn't be too strenuous.

Apart from a tendency to yawn throughout breakfast, Kelsie felt no ill-effects from her late night. The other two girls skipped breakfast in favour of a few extra minutes' sleep, but the boy, who had now lost his initial diffidence at finding himself outnumbered by the females at Knowle, was full of energy.

During the first session, he had to be gently restrained by Avril Collier.

'Not so fast, David! It's lovely to have so much enthusiasm, but you mustn't urge your rider on quite so quickly. One thing at a time, please, or he'll quickly lose confidence.'

Kelsie found pretending to be a pupil more difficult than giving instruction. She had begun by working with a woman who was supposed to be deaf, and had enjoyed the challenge of devising a means of communication with her 'guinea-pig'. Then Avril had asked her to imagine that her legs were paralysed, and a group of the students had been charged with the tricky business of negotiating her wheelchair on to a ramped mounting-block. Then they were to lift her out of the chair and on to a patient cob. Jean Lanyon had the responsibility of holding the cob steady, so Kelsie had no fears in that direction. Meanwhile, Avril was rapidly issuing instructions to the other three helpers, a girl waiting on the off-side of the cob, and David and the military man with Kelsie on the block.

'Right, Brigadier Short, you hold the chair steady. David, stand by to lift. We won't need a lot of brute strength here as Kelsie's only a slip of a thing. Rosemary, prepare to lift the right leg over gently as she comes towards you. Now, what first? That's right, Brigadier Short, brake the wheelchair and unfasten the seat-belt. No, only remove the right-hand arm-rest, then she can use the other to push herself up. . . . No, David, don't start yet. You haven't folded back the foot-rest. That's it. *No*, David! You're in too much of a hurry still. First you must ask if Kelsie's ready – she's not a sack of potatoes. Then give the agreed signal for the lift. OK. Off you go.'

It was tricky for Kelsie to keep her legs totally relaxed, but her helpers managed very well. It was a strange sensation to have her feet placed in the stirrups, and even stranger, as Mrs Lanyon led the cob away from the mounting-block, to have Rosemary at her side with a steadying hand on her belt strap gravely explaining the first principles of riding.

At the end of the session, all were agreed that they had learnt most of all from being 'guinea-pig' riders, and after coffee they prepared for their first class with the local RDA group with greater confidence.

There were six children and two adults from the group, with a variety of disabilities. They all stayed to lunch with the course members, as they were to take part in the 'Fun and Games' in the afternoon. Mounts were found for everyone, and they had a thoroughly good time trying out all sorts of games from musical posts to 'Grandmother's Hoofsteps'.

It was when she dismounted from this session that Kelsie began to feel the effects of her late night. She was elated enough to join in the final animated discussion at tea-time, but after the goodbyes had been said and they were settled in the car ready for the homeward drive, she found herself desperate for sleep.

'I'm awfully glad I haven't got to drive,' she yawned, as they left the gates of Knowle Castle behind them. 'Though I suppose I shall have to think about driving lessons next year.' She looked regretfully out at the moorland scenery. 'We never got a chance to get out on to Dartmoor proper.'

'Perhaps we'll come back for another course some day.' Mrs Lanyon turned the car on to the main road. 'I'm so pleased you enjoyed these two days as much as I did. I'm looking forward to putting all these ideas into practice, aren't you? By the way, what did you think about the lecture on special tack and equipment? I was wondering about ramps and mounting blocks . . .'

But Kelsie's head was already nodding and there was no reply. Mrs Lanyon smiled to herself. The journey home looked like being a quiet one.

By the time she had finished a very late supper in Crantock's kitchen, Kelsie had revived sufficiently to join in Mrs Lanyon's account of their two days at Knowle. Roger and Mr Lanyon listened with keen interest and asked a lot of questions. Mrs Lanyon was sorry that Toby was already in bed. He might have taken no interest if he had been there, but now he was bound to feel excluded from the enthusiastic mood brought on by the course.

'As from tomorrow, it's all systems go,' announced Mrs Lanyon. 'Next on the list is the public meeting in the village to round up support and volunteers. In the meantime – bed. Kelsie may have caught up on her beauty sleep in the car, but I haven't! Oh, I nearly forgot to ask you both how everything's been here while we've been away. I've hardly given the dear old place a thought in the last forty-eight hours.'

'Absolutely fine. Everything went like clockwork,' her husband assured her. 'By the way, Kelsie, there was a phone call for you. A female voice, but she wouldn't leave a name or a message. She seemed put out when I said you were away, but relieved when I told her you would be back this evening.'

'I wonder who that could be?' Kelsie yawned as she made for the door. 'Never mind. I expect she'll ring again if it's anything important.'

In spite of her doze in the car, Kelsie fell into a heavy sleep almost immediately. She thought briefly about the horse that might soon be hers – she must find time tomorrow to tell Roger and ask his advice – but sleep, when it came, was remarkably free of horses. Her dreams were all connected with her old life in London, running to catch trains, crowded streets, her old school.

She woke with a start in the middle of a dream about trying to capture an over-excited Ajax in the middle of a supermarket. A dim grey light was filtering through the curtains of her attic bedroom and outside were the first, hesitant notes of the dawn chorus. It was not yet five o'clock and she was wide awake. Bother. She must just turn over and go back to sleep.

Then she heard a noise; a noise that certainly should not have been heard at Crantock at a quarter to five on a June morning. It was the engine of a heavy vehicle toiling up the lane from the house to the main road. Immediately she was out of bed and peering through the window, but she could see nothing. Ajax awoke and padded over to her with a whine of enquiry.

'That's very strange.' Kelsie rubbed his ears, absentmindedly. 'I suppose it could be a milk tanker that's taken a wrong turn, eh boy?'

She was about to get back into bed when she remembered a column in last week's 'Cornishman' about modern-day cattle rustlers with lorries clearing an unsuspecting farm of its entire stock. If there were cattle thieves about, why not horse-thieves? Her throat went dry and her heart began to pound. Don't be silly, she told herself sternly. You've got horse-nappers on the brain! Nothing like that is going to happen. Distractedly she began to pull jeans and a jersey on over her pyjamas. Ajax gave a little bark and she hushed him.

'You can come with me, but I'm not waking anyone else up. I shall feel such a fool if nothing's wrong.'

All the same, when she came down the stairs to find Roger standing on the landing, she was quite relieved. Quickly she explained what had woken her.

'Heard you creaking about over my head,' he said briefly. 'Thought you were ill or something. Hang on.' In a moment he had reappeared fully dressed and they were quietly going down the stairs, Ajax at their heels, his nails scratching on the bare wood.

Once outside, they ran to the Long Meadow.

'Ranger and Columbine are by the gate,' said Roger with relief. 'And I can see Dormouse, Windswept and Jester.' Kelsie ran ahead. The light was getting stronger, and she climbed on to the stone hedge for a better view.

'Comfrey and Sam are lurking at the far end. And there's Cinders, tucked in behind Sam.'

'That's all in the Long Meadow. Now for the Five-acre.' They ran alongside the hedge to the next gate.

'Alexander, Piper, Rupert . . .' panted Kelsie.

'And there's Firecracker. Granada's in the stable but Butters and Baggins should be here.' Kelsie tipped herself over the gate and ran to the field shelter. Firecracker and Rupert skittered away from her in surprise at such early-morning antics.

'All's well!' Kelsie emerged from the shed. 'They're in here.' Roger joined her and they scrambled over the bank into the orchard.

Trust Roger *not* to make for the orchard first off, thought Kelsie, dodging between the trees.

'Stop crashing about,' ordered Roger. 'You'll frighten them.' Peering through the trees Kelsie saw what Roger's sharp eyes had already seen, the startled faces of Ladystream and Fallow looking up from an early graze. Kelsie sighed with relief, and then felt a sudden lurch of fear.

'Sorrel! Where's Sorrel?'

'Still at the stud, you fool.' Roger gave her a little push. 'She's not due back till tomorrow.'

'I forgot,' said Kelsie weakly, and leant back against a tree.

'That's all accounted for except Granada. We'd better check the stable, though it's looking as if we've had a false alarm.'

'I'm sorry,' Kelsie apologized as they crossed the yard. 'It did seem strange to hear a truck or whatever it was in the lane at that hour of the morning. Why did you bring Granada in, by the way?'

'I heard him cough a couple of times yesterday. Probably nothing, but I thought I'd separate him from the others and take a good look at him today . . . Good grief! What's that?'

A loud banging was coming from the stables. Roger and Kelsie looked at one another. Kelsie put her hand round Ajax's muzzle to tell him to be quiet, and then tip-toed after Roger to the stable door. It was open. Cautiously, they edged inside. Granada, quiet as a mouse, was standing in the first stall, looking over it with an expression of mild enquiry. The noise was coming from the end stall and was unmistakable. It was the noise of very angry hooves lashing out at wooden boards. Suddenly there was a neigh, and a head, a wicked, ugly skewbald head, reared up over the side of the stall. It was Tornado – alias Murphy – the Fury on Four Legs!

6

The Foundling

A council of war was held in the stables. The Lanyons and Kelsie gathered around the end stall while the object of their attentions made short work of a haynet. Over the side of the stall someone had hung Murphy's tack – the elaborate western saddle and an equally decorative bridle. Tucked behind the stirrup leathers, they had found a letter, and Kelsie was now reading it aloud.

'"Dear Kelsie, I tried to ring you, but you were away. Knowing how you and your friends like to rescue horses, I thought you might be willing to take on Murphy. I'm off today to join the Cirque de Zurich, but of course they only want Princess. I have tried, but I can't find a home for Murphy. The only alternative is the knacker's yard and it seems a pity. He's young and healthy and it's not his fault he's been trained into bad habits. The money is for his keep to begin with, but please consider Murphy your property from now on. Best wishes, Tara." . . . Oh, and there's a PS. "I thought you would like to have the tack. It's worth quite a lot. *Don't* use the saddle. He's only safe to ride bareback." That's all.'

Kelsie showed a clutch of five-pound notes to the

others and ran a hand through her already tousled hair.

'"Please consider Murphy your property from now on",' quoted Roger. 'What a nerve!'

'It's my own fault,' groaned Kelsie. 'I went on and on, that time at the Crow's Nest, about all the horses we'd saved from dreadful fates.'

Toby's eyes were shining.

'I think it's smashing! The best thing that's happened for ages.' He gave Murphy's flank an encouraging slap and the gelding looked round, pulling the most appalling face.

'Toby,' said his mother, quietly. 'You know what has been agreed about taking on any more lame ducks.' She looked anxious. Toby opened his mouth as if to argue, but his father forestalled him by putting an arm round his shoulders.

'Come on, Toby, just think about it for a moment. We can't jeopardize the well-being of the horses we've already got for this chap, however sad a case he is.' Murphy looked far from sad. He rolled his eyes in a comical fashion and once more gave the haynet his full attention. Evidently his display of stall-banging had been brought on by boredom and hunger.

Kelsie felt a leaden, shrinking sensation overtake her. She swallowed hard and heard herself say, as if it was somebody else, a long way off,

'It's all right, Toby. Tara's given him to me. Jean said I could have a horse of my own, so I suppose it'll have to be him.'

She regretted it immediately. As she looked at Murphy's unattractive rear end, her dream horse went galloping over a distant horizon, never to return. Four startled faces turned towards her.

'Kelsie!' exclaimed Mrs Lanyon. 'Are you serious?'

'You're mad,' stated Roger, flatly.

'Good for you!' Toby was the only one in the stable with a smiling face as Janet walked in.

'So this is where you all are. I thought the place had been deserted. Shall I start bringing the ponies in . . . Golly!' She caught sight of Murphy and recognized him immediately. 'It's Tornado!'

'Don't call him that,' protested Kelsie faintly. 'It's Murphy from now on,' she added, a little more determination in her voice.

Murphy's strange arrival was explained to Janet, who naturally thought it as exciting as Toby did.

'Fantastic! Fancy sneaking him in at dead of night. It's like finding a foundling on your doorstep.'

Roger snorted.

'Some foundling!' He turned to his father. 'Look, Dad, I'm as sorry as the next person that this creature's homeless, but do you really think we ought to let Kelsie take him on? I mean, he's not anyone's idea of an ideal mount.'

'It's Kelsie's decision.' Mr Lanyon looked at her with an enquiring smile. 'That wretched circus girl has put you in an impossible position. It's really a kind of blackmail, dumping the horse here, mentioning the knacker's yard and telling you he's all yours. I think you should make no decisions at all for the time being. We'll see if we can track down this Tara female first. She can't be allowed to off-load her responsibilities like this.'

Kelsie felt much more cheerful. She and Mr Lanyon went to the house to see if they could find a way of contacting Harvey's Circus by phone, while everyone else got down to the delayed routine of the stables.

Kelsie remembered Tara saying that the circus would be in Plymouth this month, so they began by ringing the city's Information office. From them they learned that the circus was now in Exeter. On ringing Exeter, they discovered the whereabouts of the circus and that there was no telephone on the site.

'At least we've got an address.' Mr Lanyon was relieved. 'Now we'll send a telemessage to Mr Harvey asking him to contact us – urgently.'

There could be no hope of an answer until the following day, so Kelsie went through a jittery twenty-four hours. At last, at mid-day they had a telephone call from the owner of the circus. The news was not helpful. Tara and Princess had left for the Continent the previous afternoon. Mr Harvey sounded regretful, but in no circumstances would he take Murphy back.

'It's not the kind of act I want any more – too many risks,' he explained. 'Sorry about Tara landing you with the brute. Typical of the girl. She thinks of no one but herself. The family won't forgive her for running out on us, in the middle of the season, too.'

Mr Lanyon put down the phone slowly.

'I expect you've gathered we're lumbered with this bucking bronco. What do you want to do, Kelsie? There's no earthly reason why you should feel obliged to take him on, you know.'

Kelsie had been thinking while Mr Lanyon was on the phone.

'I wouldn't like him to be put down.' She fiddled with the code book on the hall table. 'Perhaps if I kept him on probation, as it were. Tried re-schooling him. Rehabilitation, Tara called it.'

'And if he turned out to be incorrigible, then get rid of him . . .? Hmmm. I should have a word with Jean and see what she thinks.'

That evening, they looked Murphy over together. He had been turned into the small paddock near the house where he was cropping the grass eagerly.

'He certainly likes his grub.' Mrs Lanyon observed him dispassionately. 'It's a pity about his looks. His head's too big and that makes him look so unbalanced when he's moving. Still, he's got powerful hindquarters. There's a lot of strength there.' The skewbald raised his head and looked at them quizzically. 'There could even be some intelligence underneath that idiotic expression.' She regarded Kelsie seriously. 'If you want to go ahead, I'm prepared to help you all I can. If he turns out untrainable, he'll have to be destroyed. On the other hand, if we can rid him of all these wild horse delusions, then it might be possible to find him another home – though you could end up being stuck with him.'

Kelsie said nothing as Murphy ambled towards them. He looked from one to the other as if trying to decide which of the two might be the softest touch. He then butted Kelsie in the chest and nosed around her pockets. Kelsie, feeding the skewbald a piece of carrot, felt a wave of unidentifiable emotion. It would be impossible to love such a disaster of a horse, but she knew she didn't want to see him go away from Crantock in the abattoir van. She ran a hand down his thick neck.

'Let's try,' was all she said.

Over thirty members of the public turned up to Methion village hall for the open meeting to set up Crantock's Riding for the Disabled scheme. Some had been attracted by posters put up in the area and others by a short piece there had been in the local newspaper. Most had come simply because they had been asked to by the Lanyons.

On the village hall platform sat Mrs Lanyon with the regional representative of the RDA, a physiotherapist from Penloe hospital, a teacher from Greenhallow special school, and Dr Carthew, the local GP. Mrs Lanyon introduced the regional representative, who explained the aims and organization of the association and then showed a short film of some RDA groups in action.

Kelsie took a quick look around at the faces in the audience. Everyone looked interested and absorbed. Roger was working the projector and Mr Lanyon was sitting in the back row with Janet and Mrs Patterson. Toby was not there. He was training that evening with the other members of the pony club team, but Kelsie knew that he wouldn't have come, even if he'd had nothing else to do.

A spontaneous burst of applause and animated conversation greeted the end of the film. Jean Lanyon called the meeting to order.

'First of all, we have to decide if there is a need for a

branch of the RDA in this area. Now there are one or two friends with handicaps here tonight . . .' She smiled at a young woman in a wheelchair in the front row. 'And several parents who have disabled children. Perhaps they would like to give their views in a minute.' Mrs Lanyon then asked the teacher and the physiotherapist to say a few words.

Both speakers were enthusiastic about the possible benefits of riding to the children and adults in their care. Discussion then became more general and offers of help came in from all sides. Mrs Bourne-Lacey was one of the first to stand up.

'I think it is wonderful of Crantock to offer not only a venue for the rides but mounts as well . . .' There were murmurs of agreement. 'But I think it would be helpful if those of us that have suitable ponies were to lend them as well, to take the pressure off the Crantock horses. Caroline and I would be very happy to lend Gypsy. Perhaps Caroline could even join in at first, to help give the others confidence.'

'A splendid idea!' said Mrs Lanyon warmly.

One or two others then offered the use of quiet ponies and many more volunteered to help. Names and addresses were duly taken. Alf Tremellick, the landlord of the 'Rose and Crown' said he would start fund-raising, and then Kelsie was surprised to see Janet's mother with her hand tentatively raised.

'Er . . . *I* was going to volunteer to help with the fund-raising. I used to be rather good at that sort of thing . . . cake-stalls and so on.' She looked around the room nervously. 'And of course I will help Mr Tremellick in any way I can. But after seeing that wonderful film . . .' Mrs Patterson took a deep breath.

'What I'd really like to do is come along to the riding sessions and lend a hand.'

'Mum!' squeaked Janet in surprise. 'You don't know anything about horses!'

'*All* help will be gratefully received,' interjected Mrs Lanyon quickly. 'We have already got some suitably knowledgeable people on the list. I'm sure Mrs Patterson will be very good with the children, and she can pick up the 'horse sense' as she goes along. We shall need two – sometimes three – helpers per pony, remember. That's a lot of volunteers.' Mrs Lanyon looked briefly at her list.

'I think we've managed to establish two things at once here. There is definitely a need for an RDA branch in the area and we have the enthusiasm and practical help in Methion to supply that need. This is a new venture for us all, and we are all going to be learning together how to run it.'

The next twenty minutes were taken up with formalities. Copies of the Association's Group Model Constitution were circulated, and motions were proposed and carried for forming the group, joining the RDA and adopting their constitution. A committee was then proposed and voted for, and by the time coffee and biscuits were carried in from the kitchen, Mrs Lanyon found herself chairman with Mrs Bourne-Lacey as secretary and Alf Tremellick as treasurer.

'As long as we can have some of the meetings at the pub,' he beamed. 'My Amy won't stand for me having too many evenings off duty.'

As Alf left and the coffee was circulated, the level of noise rose. Mr and Mrs Lanyon were surrounded by people eager to discuss further ideas. Roger got on quietly with packing up the projector, but Kelsie was surprised to find herself surrounded by another group of Methion people, none of whom wanted, for the moment, to talk about the RDA.

If Kelsie had led a more social life in Methion or Penloe, she might have realized that she had become something of a local celebrity, simply by being Ellen Forbes's daughter. The previous month she had dutifully watched the wedding episode of 'Pringle's Parish' on the Pattersons' TV and had even bought a copy of that week's *TV Times*. There on the cover was her mother's smiling face, and behind the happy couple were the rest of the cast. In the upper left-hand corner she could just make out the top of her own head. Inside there was a big feature on 'Our Newest Serial Star', with lots of pictures of Ellen Forbes on the set of the show and in her Manchester flat.

From her mother's letters, Kelsie had gathered that she was kept busy making 'personal appearances', opening shops and fêtes and going to charity events. She had felt sorry for her mother, becoming public property, but not for one moment had she expected any of this instant fame to rub off on to herself. This evening was a revelation.

She found herself surrounded by a crowd of eager questioners. When was Ellen Forbes going to come down to Cornwall again? Could Kelsie ask for some signed photographs? Was it true Ellen really was going to marry the actor playing that nice vicar? Was there an official Ellen Forbes fan club, and if so, where did you write to?

Kelsie was bewildered. Her mother had always

been an actress, mostly in the theatre, but this was her first real success on television. It began to dawn on Kelsie, that after watching two episodes of 'Pringle's Parish' every week, these people felt they knew her mother as well as she did. She answered questions as best she could. Yes, her mother was coming down for a holiday in late September. No, as far as she knew her mother had no plans to marry again. Sorry, she didn't know anything about a fan club. She sensed their disappointment and looked round for an excuse to get away.

'Must go and help wash up,' she babbled. 'I'll see what I can do about the photographs, I promise.' She dived for the kitchen and shut the door behind her. Her head had been full of Murphy and the RDA until ten minutes ago. Now she could think only of her mother and how she was coping with all this publicity and interest in her private life. It was all very confusing.

Having got the RDA scheme off to a good start, Jean Lanyon felt able to turn her attentions to Murphy. 'The Foundling', as Toby insisted on calling him, had been checked out by the vet, and found to be sound in wind and limb.

'Not a bonny animal,' he had remarked in his dry, Scots voice. 'But strong – I'll give ye that.' Then, just as he opened his car door, he turned to say casually over his shoulder, 'By the way, this disabled riding lark of yours . . . I'll waive my consulting fee for any animal you use for it.' Brushing aside thanks, he got into his car and drove off, leaving Kelsie dancing with delight in the stable yard.

The next stage with the skewbald was to introduce him to the other horses. Noting his size, most of the ponies kept well clear of him, though he seemed to strike up a friendship with Alexander which the Lanyons felt could only be a good influence. It was Alexander who was later to give Mrs Lanyon an idea for Murphy's re-education.

Roger, who had watched the circus bronco act very carefully, came up with a heartening theory about Murphy's rearing habits.

'I think he was trained to do that on a cue,' he said one windy morning as they watched Murphy, full of high spirits, career round the Five-acre. 'Watch. He's bucking now. That's what comes naturally, and of course it'll have to be dealt with. But I haven't seen him rear since he's been here – not that we've tried him in a saddle of course. I reckon that they used drum-rolls as the trigger for rearing.'

Toby immediately dashed off to the house and returned with a battered old drum and two wooden spoons.

'Let's try with these – can't find the drum-sticks,' he panted. 'I hope I can make enough noise.'

It was quite enough for Murphy. As Toby pounded away at the drum, he lifted his head and went into a spectacular rear, neighing at the top of his voice.

'There!' Toby was triumphant. 'Roger's right – oh, hell, I've split the drum skin!'

'Never mind.' Mrs Lanyon seemed pleased. 'We've proved a point. We can easily keep him away from drums for the time being. It may be something he'll grow out of anyway, when he's been away from the circus for long enough. Now, to get rid of this bucking nonsense.'

'He's fine without a saddle, we know that,' pointed out Kelsie. 'I rode him bareback for nearly an hour yesterday and he was as good as gold. Jolly uncomfortable gait he's got, though.'

'All that tearing about in the confined space of the circus ring wouldn't have helped.'

Roger had another idea.

'Do you think that Tara played the old gorse trick on him?'

'What's that?' Kelsie wanted to know.

'Sprigs of gorse under the saddle,' explained Roger, briefly. 'No more than uncomfortable at first, but the minute anyone gets into the saddle, the horse will do anything to get rid of the pressure.'

'That's terrible.' Kelsie was appalled. 'Tara couldn't have been so cruel.'

'After a while you don't need to use the gorse. Just the weight on his back is all that is needed to drive the horse berserk.'

'However the damage was done, we've got to undo it,' said Mrs Lanyon with determination. 'A horse that can't be ridden with a saddle is not a lot of use to Kelsie. So we'll start lunging him, with a saddle and fixed side reins crossed over the withers to prevent him getting his head down to buck. It'll give a better carriage to that heavy head of his. Kelsie will do the lunging, as it's her voice he must learn to answer. The lunge will help him with free forward movement, too. It's worth spending a lot of time on.'

So every evening, Kelsie, Mrs Lanyon and

Murphy met in the small paddock to work on the lunge. To everyone's amazement, Murphy made splendid progress. He produced no unpleasant tricks and his ungainly stride began to improve almost immediately. There appeared to be plenty of brains inside the ugly head.

Kelsie began to feel much more hopeful about her unwanted protégé. It was good to have a horse that was her own responsibility, even if he was very unlikely ever to be a credit to his owner. The thought of being seen with him in public made Kelsie shudder.

One fine evening, when Kelsie had just returned from Penloe College, where she had been making some final preparations for re-taking her O-levels, she decided to take the skewbald for a quiet hack into the woods. She went to the tack-room to collect the bridle, hesitated a moment and then took down the western saddle as well. She led Murphy into the yard and tacked him up. He didn't even flicker his white eyelashes as she slid the heavy saddle on to his back and fastened the girths. Kelsie talked to him soothingly. She told him that she had been riding him bare-back for some weeks now, that she was a light-weight rider and that he was a good, *good* boy.

Almost without realizing it, she was in the saddle. Murphy stood stock still as she gathered up the reins, and Kelsie let out a sigh of relief. Then Murphy began to buck – half-heartedly at first, which gave Kelsie a moment to grasp the pommel, but then with increasing energy. Off! Off! OFF! he seemed to be screaming silently with every buck. The stable buildings lurched around them at amazing angles. Kelsie clenched her teeth and hung on for dear life.

It was a buck combined with a massive swerve that brought her off. Knowing it was a long way to fall and the ground was hard, she managed to cling to the saddle for a moment before pushing herself away from the gelding's plunging body. She landed on her feet, then her knees before rolling awkwardly sideways.

'Bravo!' came a voice from the stable office door. Roger's clapping was sardonic. As Kelsie struggled to her feet he crossed the yard towards her. Murphy had stopped cavorting and was regarding them both with a clownish expression.

'Trying to be Tara Mark Two?' Roger enquired coldly. 'Not succeeding very well, are we?'

Rage bubbled up inside Kelsie, whether with Roger, Murphy or herself, she didn't know. Breathing heavily, she caught Murphy's reins and, limping slightly, led him towards the stable. As she passed Roger, she said in as dignified a tone as she could muster,

'Sometimes, Roger Lanyon, you are an unmitigated prig!'

7

Progress

Roger stared at Kelsie for a moment. Then his face broke into a smile.

'Only when *you're* an unmitigated idiot,' he laughed, ruffling her hair. 'Here, I'll see to the Terrible Tornado, while you go and have a bath. There's plenty of witch-hazel for your bruises in the medicine cabinet!'

Without another word, Kelsie handed over the reins and made for the house. It was difficult to be angry with a Lanyon for very long.

At supper, she confessed her ill-advised experiment to Mrs Lanyon, who didn't waste time with recriminations. She was much more interested in Murphy's behaviour.

'So he didn't go mad straight away? That could be a good sign. But I've been thinking anyway that the only way to cure him is to teach him that however much he bucks, he is *not* going to get rid of his rider.'

'How do we do that? He got rid of me quite easily. I don't suppose you want to have a go?' Kelsie looked at Mrs Lanyon hopefully.

'No, I do not.' Mrs Lanyon laughed. 'I can't possibly run a school with broken bones. But I did have an idea this afternoon, while I was taking out a ride on Alexander. You remember he came from an old lady who used to hunt him right up to her death at the age of seventy-one? Of course, she rode side-saddle. Now, provided the girth or balance-straps don't break and the horse doesn't fall down, it is almost impossible to come off riding side-saddle.'

'Really?' Kelsie was immediately interested.

'Well, riding astride with a bucker your seat naturally leaves the saddle. Side-saddle you can sit right down, really screw your knees into the pommel and defy him to get you off.'

'Have we still got one, Mum?' Roger asked.

'Yes, we've still got Alex's somewhere.'

'But I've never ridden side-saddle!' put in Kelsie.

'Then now's the time to learn,' said Mrs Lanyon, bracingly. 'But on Alexander. It'll be a while before we allow Murphy the indulgence of another bucking bronco act.'

All Kelsie's spare time at the moment was supposed to be given over to revision for her Maths, French and Geography exams. Learning to ride side-saddle however, seemed to be an urgent priority, if she was ever going to get the measure of Murphy, so revision slipped into the background. To begin with, Jean insisted on short sessions with the old hunter on the lunge, until Kelsie had become used to the new position. Once she had mastered the knack of taking all her weight on the right seatbone and thigh, together with the characteristic twist of the rib-cage that brings the spine in line with the horse's, the whole business seemed easier.

Kelsie felt even better when one day Mrs Bourne-Lacey turned up at Crantock with a riding habit.

'It was my grandmother's. She would have been so pleased to know that a youngster like you was riding side-saddle. Please have it. I know it will look lovely.'

Even Roger was approving when Kelsie took her first ride off the lunge, wearing the elegant grey skirt and jacket.

'Very smart!' he called across the Long Meadow from the orchard where he was talking to Sorrel. 'You can show one of the mares for me at the County show next year.'

'I'll hold you to that.' Kelsie sent Alexander into a smooth canter. She was enjoying herself. It was the next stage of Mrs Lanyon's plan that she was not looking forward to – trying the side-saddle on Murphy.

July seemed to go by in a flash. Kelsie continued to ride the hunter and lunge Murphy. The dreaded O-levels were duly taken, but were somehow less momentous because of all the hard work going on at Crantock. Mrs Lanyon tied up the formalities over forming the Methion RDA group while Alf Tremellick and the Pattersons organized a Summer Fayre in the village to raise money for mounting blocks and neck-straps. Sorrel and Ladystream were both in foal, but Roger was showing Fallow in some yearling classes. Toby was entirely absorbed in the pony club jumping team, and with fitting out a dark room in the attic so that he could develop his own films.

Even Janet had her own scheme – to turn her mother into a fit RDA helper. Whenever she had one of the Crantock ponies for a hack she insisted that her mother came too, walking alongside for most of the way while Janet lectured her on horse management. Mrs Patterson even found herself tacking-up and cleaning, and in spite of a few broken finger-nails found herself enjoying it.

Meanwhile, Kelsie's mother was a subject of concern at Crantock. Hardly a week went by without some reference to her in the popular press, and Kelsie had received some irritating calls from local journalists 'looking for a story'.

One evening, while she was lunging Murphy with the side-saddle on his back, her mother rang from Manchester. Handing over the rein to Roger, Kelsie rushed to the telephone.

'Mum! What's all this rubbish in the paper about "Confessions of a TV Star"?' were her first words.

'Nauseating, isn't it?' Ellen Forbes sounded depressed. 'Pure invention, love, by a revolting gossip columnist I refused to talk to. This so-called exclusive interview is her way of getting her own back. Try not to take any notice.'

'All right . . . but none of it sounds like *you*. I wish I could see you soon. When are you coming down for a holiday?'

'Not until late September or early October, I'm afraid.' Kelsie was disappointed.

'There's so much to tell you and show you . . . yes, Murphy's coming on very well. The saddler has made Alexander's side-saddle fit him and added a quick-release stirrup for safety. A lot of Tara's money went on it, but it's important he should feel comfortable. Oh, but wait till you see him – he's a horror!'

Mother and daughter chatted on, regardless of time, until Ellen Forbes remembered some more news.

'The reason I can't take a holiday until late September is that I'm having a week off this month to go to London. I'm making a series of commercials for a floor polish . . . Don't laugh, Kelsie! I'm afraid it will make me even more of a household name.' She sighed and then added more brightly, 'But it's all part of a plan, Kelsie. I'll explain when I see you. I may have sorted myself out by then.'

Kelsie put the phone down feeling slightly mystified, but her mother's vague hints were soon forgotten with the beginning of the holidays.

The riding school was busier than ever, and every day there was Murphy's training to be fitted in. Then there were pony club events and the local shows and gymkhanas. Time also had to be found for Janet's driving lessons. Just for fun, Janet had entered a driving class at Penloe show for 'commercial vehicles'. Roger and Kelsie re-painted the jingle in red and black with 'Crantock Free-range Eggs' on the back in yellow letters. Janet was overcome with excitement and pleasure, and in her enthusiasm managed to persuade her mother to ride as a passenger in the class. Partly because there were only a few entries, they returned in triumph, Piper's bridle bearing a green rosette.

The highlight of August this year was not the show, however, it was the start of RDA sessions. The children from Greenhallow would not be coming until the autumn term, but Mrs Lanyon was happy to begin with a small group of local disabled people.

The first step was for the would-be-riders to be brought to Crantock for a visit. All the helpers were there to meet them and show them around. They were introduced to the ponies and encouraged to stroke them and give them tit-bits. Caroline and Gypsy then gave a demonstration ride round the paddock, and then back at the stable yard Comfrey, Butterscotch and Dormouse were tacked up, complete with new neck-straps. Three brave volunteer visitors were then kitted out with hats and safety-belts and slowly and carefully helped to mount.

All the ponies behaved beautifully with the specially-made mounting block with its ramp for wheelchairs, but they had been given some practice with it beforehand. Only one of the volunteers was in a wheelchair, Jimmy, a boy with spina bifida from Penloe. He had been brought by his physiotherapist, who carefully watched as he was eased into the saddle. The three were then led round the paddock, helpers on either side, for a few circuits before a happy return to the yard.

There was only one small moment of anxiety as they came through the gate when Jimmy lifted both hands in triumph to wave to a friend. Strong arms came up on each side to steady him, while Comfrey's leader halted the pony.

'I think "look, no hands!" is a bit advanced for the first ride, Jimmy,' Mrs Lanyon called out gaily, and the three pioneers were dismounted amid laughter.

After squash and biscuits in the garden, the visitors left Crantock looking forward eagerly to their first proper session.

This was to be held on August 7th, and help and transport were duly arranged. Toby was furious.

'Didn't you remember that it's the semi-finals of the jumping?' he demanded when he found out. 'I suppose the lot of you will be too busy to come and watch me and Firecracker!' Everyone was genuinely sorry, but it was too late to change the date, and so Toby felt more disgruntled than ever.

August 7th dawned cloudless and warm and Crantock hummed with expectation. A friend's horse-box came to collect Toby and Firecracker early in the morning, and the others set about their daily tasks and preparations for the afternoon. Mrs Lanyon and Kelsie pored over the stable planner, trying to decide which of the suitable ponies and horses could be used that afternoon.

'They've all been so busy, that's the trouble,' sighed Jean Lanyon. 'Still, we only have eight riders coming, and helpers are bringing two horses strong enough for adults – that's Dr Carthew's Taffy, and Bowler, that's the big brown gelding belonging to the Nances. Windswept and Jester will do nicely for the other two adults. We've a six year old – the little girl with lung trouble, so we must have Cinders.'

'Butterscotch was awfully good at the trial session,' remarked Kelsie.

'Yes, but he's so popular in the school that he's been worked hard this week. I think we'll have to use Piper, Dormouse and Columbine.'

They were due to start at two-fifteen and by two o'clock the yard was full of helpers. Mrs Lanyon and Kelsie were with them, issuing explanations and instructions while Roger, Mr Lanyon and Janet were tacking up the Crantock mounts. The helpers were now all familiar faces to Kelsie, and she was particularly pleased to see Mrs Patterson in trousers and shiny new wellingtons leading out Cinders with great confidence. She nudged Janet.

'Your mother's coming on. Bet you get your pony after all.'

'I'm working on it.' Janet sounded hopeful. 'Hey, look! We've got customers.' A mini-bus had drawn into the car-park and a ramp was being let down at the back.

'Jimmy's in there.' Roger strolled towards them. 'You should see his face. He can't wait to get out of the bus!'

After some basic instruction from Mrs Lanyon in the small paddock, they all went for a gentle walk along the track into the woodland that now belonged to their neighbour, Colonel Standish. He was with them as a volunteer, leading the sturdy hunter, Bowler. It was a beautiful afternoon, not too hot or plagued by flies, and Kelsie felt at peace with the world as she walked with Mrs Patterson alongside Cinders.

The Shetland's rider was a pretty child, pale with long fair hair. It was hard to remember that she was suffering from a disease that could be a killer.

'You're doing very well, Emma,' encouraged Kelsie. 'Try and keep your back a bit straighter . . . that's it.' At one point they broke into a trot, Mrs Patterson's arm firmly round Emma, in order to catch up with the larger pony in front.

'Sorry, that was a bit bumpy,' apologized Kelsie,

'but Cinders hates to be left behind. And of course she takes about four strides to everyone else's one.'

'That's all right,' said Emma seriously. 'The more joggling about I do the better. Then they won't have to bang my back so much when I have my physiotherapy.'

'You wait till we really learn to trot, then,' Kelsie promised. 'You'll get all the joggling about you want!'

Kelsie fell silent as Mrs Patterson began to chat to Emma. Mrs Lanyon was anxious not to rush the new riders. There would be plenty of time to work towards the exercises and games. For the moment it was enough to look back at the other smiling faces. Jimmy was gazing round at the trees with an expression of wonder on his face. He seemed particularly thrilled as Dormouse splashed through the stream. Kelsie smiled to herself. Of course. This was hardly the kind of place he could ever have visited in a wheelchair.

When they got back to Crantock, Kelsie was surprised to see another boy in a wheelchair waiting with the mini-bus driver. Later, when the visitors had gone and the helpers were crowded into the kitchen for a cup of tea and to talk over the success of the afternoon, Kelsie sought out Mrs Lanyon to ask her about the child.

'Apparently that's Jimmy's best friend. His name is Douglas and he's very severely disabled – no control of arms or legs – and the physiotherapist feels it would be impossible to keep him safely in the saddle. He hates to be separated from Jimmy and came along today for the outing.'

'It seems an awful shame.' Kelsie was troubled.

Then Janet joined the conversation.

'If you're talking about Douglas, I had an idea about him. Couldn't we at least use the jingle to take him for rides?'

'Of course we could! That's a brilliant idea,' approved Kelsie.

Mrs Lanyon thought for a moment.

'We would need to pad the seat and put in a proper support for his back. Probably some kind of safety strap as well. I'm sure it could be done. I'll ask Hugh if he could fix something up soon, while we've still some money in the kitty. I wouldn't like to see Douglas sitting on the sidelines for too long.'

It was an idea that was put to Mr Lanyon that evening. The family had been careful to listen attentively to Toby's account of his successful day with the Pony Club, but had eventually succumbed to the temptation of discussing their RDA afternoon in detail. Toby immediately got up and left the room.

Mrs Lanyon looked irritated.

'I'm beginning to lose patience with Toby. He's behaving like a spoilt brat.'

'Perhaps he's regretting being left out,' suggested Roger. Kelsie sighed.

'I wish he'd been there this afternoon. It wasn't quite complete without Toby.'

The Methion branch had three more sessions in August, and so much progress was made that everyone looked forward to the start of the autumn term when ten children from Greenhallow would come for a later lesson on Monday afternoons. Janet and two other pupils from Crantock managed to get permission from their schools to continue to help in term-time.

'He agreed that it was a community service,' Janet explained to her mother. 'Anyway, I'm only missing games and needlework. You didn't really need a gingham apron with embroidered pockets anyway, did you?'

Not only were her O-level results due, but the beginning of September was to be the time for Kelsie to try riding Murphy with the side-saddle. She was dreading it. It was all very well to tell herself that she would simply stay on until Murphy got tired of bucking and gave up.

'He's a strong horse,' she pointed out to Roger as she saddled the skewbald on the fateful day. 'He might never get tired. I bet my legs give in before his do.'

'Rubbish!' said Roger with easy optimism. 'You'll be fine.' Kelsie felt slightly sick as she led Murphy into the small paddock. All the Lanyons and Janet were leaning over the rails.

'This isn't a rodeo, you know,' she muttered as she passed them.

'Cheer up, Kelsie,' encouraged Mr Lanyon.

'Just remember everything we've said about him.' Mrs Lanyon's voice was matter-of-fact. 'You'll be more than a match for Murphy, now that we've got to know him.'

Toby sat himself on the top rail.

'I wanted to bring out all the mattresses and put them round the paddock for you, but they wouldn't let me.'

'Thanks for nothing,' Kelsie returned. Roger came up the other side of Murphy's head.

'Would you like me to try instead?' he asked quietly.

'No, thanks. It's got to be me.' Kelsie stopped and looked Murphy in the eye. 'Well, my lad. This is it.' Murphy snorted, stamped a forefoot and butted Kelsie in the stomach.

'Ow. Stop it. Definitely no Polos now until this is all over.'

It was important that Kelsie should be securely in the saddle before the fun began, so Roger held the horse firmly under his whiskery chin and talked to him soothingly, while Kelsie eased herself into the saddle, no mean feat when you are short in the leg and your mount is over sixteen hands. Once she was comfortably in position with her right leg hooked safely over the top pommel, Roger stepped back, still talking to Murphy, whose large ears were twitched well forward to listen.

The watchers at the gate held their breath. Murphy seemed to consider for a moment. Then he rolled his little eyes and laid back his ears. As soon as the ears came back, Kelsie was ready for him. She turned her left toe down, bringing the thigh up hard under the bottom pommel, and drew back her right heel towards her left shin, screwing herself down into the saddle.

'Let's go, Murphy,' she said loudly. And go he did.

There was not one square inch of the paddock that Murphy did not cover in his attempts to dislodge his burden. At first he seemed to buck in bursts of three, a pause between each burst, as if wondering why he hadn't managed to get rid of his rider. Then he began a sustained series of bucks, designed to show everyone that he was not to be trifled with.

Kelsie found this no worse than she had expected, and it was certainly true that the side-saddle was proving its worth. There was one terrible, stomach-lurching moment when the skewbald seemed to disappear from under her, sideways, but it was an illusion. Horse and rider were still firmly glued together.

Murphy paused for a moment in his mad display and looked around the paddock. No spotlight, no music, no catcalls and cheers. What was going on? This breathing-space gave Kelsie an opportunity she had been waiting for. She instructed him to walk on. Unfortunately, walking was the last thing on Murphy's mind at that moment. He leaped forward like a rocking-horse and began to buck again with renewed determination.

Kelsie was aware that she was breathing deeply, her heart was pounding as if she had been running uphill, her thighs were aching – and she would very much like it to be all over. The Lanyons were only a few yards away, but she was beginning to feel very lonely, perched up on this great, ugly scarecrow of a horse with his humorous expressions and his far from funny habits.

The acrobatics came to another momentary halt. This was better. Murphy trotted a few steps and she began to turn him in a circle. Then in a split second, the skewbald had flung himself forward and they were right on top of the Lanyons. She caught their expressions of horror as they tumbled off the fence.

Murphy was slamming himself against the rails in his attempts to be rid of her. Fortunately it was his off-side and Kelsie's legs were safely arranged on the other. With a great effort of will she turned him to the centre of the paddock, where he performed several minutes' worth of bucks, 'rather like clockwork running down', as Toby commented afterwards.

Exhausted, and longing to dismount, Kelsie nevertheless realized that Murphy himself was tiring. At the first opportunity, she persuaded him to canter in a passable circle. It was Murphy's best pace, and apart from a couple of token bucks on the way, he continued for another minute in good grace. Roger then opened the paddock gate and Kelsie took the skewbald once round the yard before bringing him to a halt. The Lanyons followed at a discreet distance and were relieved to find Kelsie still aloft, as the horse stood in the yard, blowing noisily, but otherwise looking reasonably harmless.

Without a word, Kelsie slid from the saddle and produced the packet of Polos.

'Go on, praise him!' urged Mrs Lanyon. Kelsie fed Murphy a second mint, then slid her arms round his neck, resting her head against his massive shoulder.

'You pig,' was all she said.

8
The Canyon

August had been a hot and dry month, and Crantock's pastures were looking brown and parched except for the two fields on either side of the stream. The beginning of September brought no change in the weather. Everyone was a little tired after the busy summer, but the children from Greenhallow school brought a new lease of life to the stables. Some were very lively and demanded constant attention from their helpers. Others were very withdrawn and needed a lot of encouragement. All of them, however, were delighted by the ponies and Mrs Lanyon was confident that they made a good start. The Methion RDA branch was now in full swing.

Roger, Toby and Kelsie were all feeling pleased with themselves, but for different reasons. Fallow had attracted a lot of attention and done well at Penloe Show, the Pony Club jumping team had had a successful season and Kelsie had passed her O-levels with surprisingly good grades.

There had been a few minor worries along the way. Baggins and Jester had been plagued by sweet-itch. Ajax had gone missing for two days, during which time Kelsie convinced herself that he had been run over. He had returned looking fit and well, though he had rushed at his feeding bowl as soon as he got inside the house. Finding it empty, he pushed aside the protesting cats and devoured their communal breakfast in two gulps. Crantock's septic tank had given some cause for concern and the old refrigerator gave up the ghost on one particularly sweltering day, but otherwise life was felt to be pretty good. Toby reluctantly started a new term, now joined on the seniors' bus by Janet, starting her first term at the comprehensive. Meanwhile, everyone waited for a break in the weather.

It seemed as if it would never come. Day after day was cloudless and warm. It didn't seem like September at all. Only the plaintive falling notes of the starlings reminded Kelsie that autumn should be on its way. The septic tank continued to smell, but the sweet-itch cleared up and Ajax showed no further inclination to roam. The horses began to look lethargic or irritable according to temperament. Only Murphy seemed to flourish in the heat.

He seemed to like a lot of exercise. Several times Kelsie had hacked him all the way to Penloe sands. On these occasions she always rode bare-back, for fear of spoiling the side-saddle she said, but really because she knew that her appearance on the beach in a riding habit would be bound to attract attention. As it was, she often felt as if all eyes were on her as she gave Murphy his head along the shore-line. His size, markings and plain ugliness made people look up from their sun-bathing as he steamed past.

One day Kelsie met Jane with her cob on the sands.

'Golly,' said Jane immediately. 'The Fury on Four Legs! Janet told me, but I could hardly believe it. I wouldn't get on that thing again for a million pounds.'

'He's fine now, honestly,' reported Kelsie. 'As long as you ride him bare-back or side-saddle. Everyone's been riding him at Crantock – Jean, Roger, Toby . . . and not a single buck.'

'Roger riding side-saddle!' hooted Jane. 'This I must see.'

'We're going to try an ordinary saddle soon; not the western one, it's too heavy. Jean reckons he's nearly sorted out. Not that he'll ever be a hundred per cent reliable, I suppose.'

Jane surveyed horse and rider critically.

'You really are over-horsed you know. He's hardly the right mount for you. You're too short in the leg.'

'I look better in the side-saddle,' returned Kelsie, rather stiffly. 'At least, so Roger says.'

'Keep your hair on,' admonished Jane, with a grin. 'It looks as if you must be getting quite fond of this delinquent animal, if you're so ready to leap to his defence.'

As Jane sent the cob into a stately canter in the opposite direction, Kelsie thought it over. Fond of Murphy? Well, perhaps. She certainly thought about him a lot. And he made her laugh. With people, you couldn't dislike someone who made you laugh. So in an odd sort of way she must be rather fond of him. He seemed to like her, too. He was always pleased to see her, easy to catch and eager to obey his newly-learned commands, despite his considerable strength and high spirits. Murphy might never win any prizes for looks or grace, but he seemed to have left his Tornado days behind him.

In the evening of another relentlessly hot day, Kelsie was sitting on the window-seat of her attic bedroom, a kitten on her lap. It had been an exhausting Monday. The blacksmith had been in the morning and there had been two RDA sessions in the afternoon. The jingle, fitted with its new seat, had made its first outing with Douglas, and that had been a great success, but one of the Greenhallow children had thrown a screaming tantrum. Her teacher had calmly got the situation under control, but not before the class had been upset and some of the ponies put on edge. For the first time Kelsie had found the session hard work instead of fun.

Now, for a while, she had Crantock to herself. Mr and Mrs Lanyon were out to supper with friends, Roger was in Penloe and Toby had gone for a ride on the Carn.

It was while they were turning out the horses that he had asked to borrow Murphy.

'Firecracker needs resting and Mum says Piper and the others should have a break, too. Murphy hasn't been out at all today, has he?' Kelsie had felt doubtful.

'No . . . but you will take care, won't you, Toby? Side-saddle or bare-back. I know he was fine yesterday when I rode astride, but that was only the first time and we shouldn't take any chances.'

'Bare-back it'll be. I'm going up on the Carn to take some photos of the sunset and I might meet someone. Side-saddle, indeed!' Toby was outraged.

'I thought you'd only got black and white film at the moment?'

'You don't have to have colour for sunsets – it's not the *colour* I'm after.'

'Well, don't forget Murphy's very strong. He pulls sometimes.'

'Oh, come on, Kelsie!' Toby sighed with impatience. 'Can I have him or can't I? You let me ride him last Sunday.'

'Yes, but Roger was with you . . . Oh, all right. Don't look at me like that. Anything for a quiet life. It's too hot to argue.'

Now, as she watched the shadows lengthen across the stable yard, she wondered if she had done the right thing. Then the kitten distracted her attention by trying to mountaineer up her bare arm. She dumped it on the floor. But after several unsuccessful attempts to leap up onto the window-seat it mewed so piteously that Kelsie had to pick it up again.

'You daft nuisance,' she said fondly, depositing him on a cushion and picking up her book.

She had hardly read half a page when the sound of hoof-beats cantering along the lane at the side of the house made her look up. She was just in time to see Murphy flash past the stable-yard gate and take a flying leap over into the Long Meadow. It was a jump worthy of a steeple-chaser.

'Toby should have seen that jump,' was the thought that flashed through Kelsie's brain in the split second before the shock-wave hit her.

Murphy was riderless. His broken reins dangled from the bit as he trotted in a disorientated way into the middle of the field. The room seemed to heave and sway as Kelsie dropped her book and threw herself at the door. It was a miracle that she didn't fall, as she took the stairs three at a time, flung open the front door and ran into the yard. Ajax, who had been draped over the tack-room steps, ran towards her, barking with excitement, but Kelsie ignored him and ran full tilt for the Long Meadow. Heart thumping, she clambered over the granite hedge, losing her balance in her haste and falling full length on to the dusty turf.

The fall brought her to her senses. What was she going to do? Toby must have been thrown, but was he even now trudging furiously along the lane, or was he lying injured among the gorse and boulders of Methion Carn? Kelsie picked herself up and walked towards Murphy. The best way of searching the Carn was on horseback. There was always the chance that having thrown Toby, the skewbald would throw her, too, but it would waste precious minutes to catch and tack up one of the other horses.

'Murphy!' she called, and her voice sounded high and strange. The skewbald looked back over his shoulder, turned and obediently trotted towards her, the broken reins swinging dangerously. She caught at them and led him through the gate. As always without a saddle, Kelsie had to take a flying leap to heave herself up on to Murphy's back. Feverishly she knotted the reins, then urged him into a fast canter along the track up to the Carn, all the time hoping to see Toby's sturdy figure marching towards her.

Never had Murphy behaved so well. He sidled into the last gate for Kelsie to open it like a nicely schooled hack. Once out onto the Carn, Kelsie looked anxiously about her. It was indeed a spectacular sunset, with the massive boulders etched against a lurid sky of pink and orange. There was not a soul to be seen. She sent Murphy straight up the track to the Giant's Thumb-ring. From there she would be able to see most of the Carn. Once there, they walked around the outside of the Ring, Kelsie scanning the horizon in all directions.

At last she could see people. There seemed to be quite a crowd of figures down by the Canyon, picnickers or walkers, perhaps. They might have seen Toby. Murphy picked his way carefully down the slope. This path was narrow and littered with loose stones. Once on the flat again, they sped towards the Canyon. As they drew closer, Kelsie could see that it was a group of young hikers clustered around the entrance with their backs towards her. They turned around at the sound of Murphy's drumming hooves.

'Hi!' she called as the gelding skidded to a halt. 'Have you seen a . . .' Her voice trailed away as she caught sight of the object of their attentions. On the well-worn path between the walls of granite was a pile of jackets and anoraks. From the nearest end protruded a pair of dirty trainers. Kelsie's throat tightened with fear. She dismounted and pushed her way through the hikers, leaving Murphy standing like a statue.

At the other end of the pile of clothes was a boy's head, his face pale and his eyes closed.

'Toby,' said Kelsie flatly, staring down at him. A young man in a red shirt standing beside her said quickly, 'You know him?' She nodded, dumbly.

'Someone's gone back to the road to stop a car and get to a phone. An ambulance should be here soon.' Kelsie nodded again, still staring down at Toby, but too shocked to speak.

'We haven't moved him,' a sandy-haired girl told her, 'in case he's broken something. None of us are medical types, I'm afraid. We know he has to be kept warm.'

'Yes,' said Kelsie. She herself began to feel icy cold. The lump in her throat felt as though it would choke her and she began to shiver. The young man took a sweater from Toby's pile.

'He's got enough to near suffocate him. Here.' He put it round her shoulders. 'You've had a shock.'

'He *is* breathing?' Kelsie's voice was low.

'What? Oh yes, first thing we checked. Heart-beat too. I'm, sure he'll be OK . . . Listen! What's that?' They all lifted their heads, and two of the group went through to the other end of The Canyon. The wail of the siren got louder as one of them shouted back,

'It's the ambulance all right. It's stopped by the gate.' Soon the ambulance men were coming through the Canyon with a stretcher.

'A nasty fall. Good thing he was wearing a hard hat', commented one of the men, as the other carefully arranged a red blanket around Toby. As he gently lifted an arm, Kelsie could see it was grazed all the way down.

'My horse threw him,' whispered Kelsie, as if she had suddenly realized it for the first time. She looked round for Murphy. He was standing where she had left him, head down at the turf.

'I must go with Toby. There will be things they need to know at the hospital.'

'That's right, love,' agreed the ambulance man. 'And he might come to on the way, and be glad of a familiar face.' The man in the red shirt came forward and offered to ride the horse back to wherever he came from.

'No!' Kelsie almost shouted. 'He's not safe. You must lead him.' As the stretcher was lifted and carried through the Canyon, she quickly gave directions to the hiker.

'Turn him into the field nearest the house and hang the bridle on the gate, please. And if there's anyone about – break it to them gently.' She handed back the sweater and ran after the stretcher, catching up with it at the gate on to the road.

Toby did not come round in the ambulance, and once at the hospital, Kelsie was distressed to find herself led into an office while Toby was wheeled down a long corridor in the opposite direction.

'Don't worry, dear,' urged the sister, sitting her down. 'He's in good hands now. You can help best by telling me his name and address so that we can contact his parents.'

Kelsie explained that Mr and Mrs Lanyon were with friends and gave the address. Then she sat in a daze as the sister made the phone call. As she put the receiver down, the nurse looked at her closely.

'They'll be here directly. Now, a cup of tea for you, young lady. You look all in.'

It was dark by this time, and the bright fluorescent light in the office was making Kelsie's eyes ache. Her head ached too, from the endless re-creation of the evening's events. It was her fault. Everything was her fault. Whichever way you looked at it, she should never have allowed Toby to take Murphy out by himself. Murphy . . . Tornado . . . She remembered her first sight of him, his frantic display in the ring. Unrideable, untameable, the showman had boasted. But even then he had not seemed vicious, just an overgrown young animal, full of high spirits and energy.

Kelsie thought again of Toby. If only he had opened his eyes . . . made a sound . . . moved a finger. She sipped the hot tea without noticing its unaccustomed sweetness. The sister had disappeared. How long had she been in this office? Surely the Lanyons must be here by now? She looked at the clock on the wall. Nearly nine o'clock. Only a couple of hours ago she had been sitting with the kitten at the window without a care in the world, and now . . .

She jumped up as the door opened. It was Roger.

'Here you are,' he said with relief. 'This place is a rabbit warren.' The normality of his voice and appearance was reassuring.

'Where are Jean and Hugh?' Kelsie fought back a sob.

'Gone straight up to see Toby. He's in intensive care.'

'Has he come round yet?'

'No, but we saw a doctor as soon as we got here. Your hiker caught me at Crantock by the way, so I biked straight back to Penloe and met Mum and Dad coming in the gates.'

'What did the doctor say?' persisted Kelsie.

'Not much,' Roger had to admit. 'They've been taking X-rays. He didn't talk as if Toby was . . . well, on the danger list.'

'But "intensive care". That sounds awful.' Kelsie was at the end of her tether. She began to sway, clutching hold of the back of the chair for support. Instantly Roger was beside her.

'Come on, Coppernob,' he said gently. It was a nickname he hadn't used for years. 'I'm taking you home.'

The next week was a living nightmare. Toby was in a coma, and Mr and Mrs Lanyon spent all their time at his bedside, waiting for him to regain consciousness. Mr Lanyon always came home at night to reassure the others and to take back news of Crantock to Jean, who slept at the hospital.

'It's a wonderful ward,' he told Roger and Kelsie. 'They're very kind to us. Everything possible is being done for Toby.'

This was little comfort to Kelsie. She went around the stables in an acute state of misery. She couldn't bear the sight of Murphy, so Roger turned him into the top field out of the way, checking the skewbald himself when they did the rounds of the other horses.

The routine of the stables had to go on. It would have been impossible for Roger and Kelsie to manage for long by themselves, but they found themselves surrounded by willing helpers.

Jane came over from Tolwidden, as soon as she heard the news, to help with classes. The trouble with Jane was that she wouldn't stop talking about the accident.

'And what are you going to do with that brute of a horse now?' she demanded. 'I should get rid of him at once if I were you. Shall I ring the vet for you? These things are better got over quickly.' Kelsie, whose private thoughts had been running along much the same lines, was amazed when Roger intervened.

'No one's ringing the vet yet. We don't know for sure that Murphy was responsible for Toby's accident.' Kelsie stared at him. 'Well, we don't,' continued Roger. 'No one *saw* it happen.' Jane opened her mouth to argue, but Roger overrode her. 'Innocent until proved guilty, that's the law with people. I know Mother would say we shouldn't treat horses worse than humans. We'll just wait and see what Toby has to say. He's the chief witness.' Kelsie felt oddly comforted by Roger's arguments, although she herself knew Murphy must be guilty.

Mrs Bourne-Lacey and Mrs Patterson were more tactful helpers, and very useful in the day-to-day running of the school. Mrs Patterson manned the telephone, which was constantly ringing with bookings and calls from well-wishers.

'I'm enjoying myself,' she confided to Roger, 'and at the same time I'm preventing Janet from playing truant from school to be here.'

As soon as school was over, Janet arrived and she, her mother, and Mrs Bourne-Lacey held the fort while Roger and Kelsie drove to the hospital.

Every time they pushed through the swing doors of the intensive care unit, Kelsie prayed that there would be good news, but for six days there was no change. Toby lay propped on the pillows, looking small and defenceless surrounded by the trappings of modern hospital equipment. The family had been told that it was a good idea to talk to Toby as if he could hear, so Roger always sat down beside the bed and launched into an account of the day's happenings. By Sunday, Kelsie found this unbearable and after a while she retreated to the waiting area with Mrs Lanyon.

Jean was looking terrible, thought Kelsie. Everything about her seemed to have faded. Her eyes, her hair, her voice. She had even lit a cigarette. Kelsie was appalled. She had never seen Mrs Lanyon smoke before.

They sat side by side on a bench-seat looking towards the glass cubicle where Toby lay and talked in low voices of Crantock. Mrs Lanyon never mentioned the accident itself and never had she suggested by a look or word that Kelsie was in any way to blame, but Kelsie herself felt heavy with guilt. The life of the ward went on around them, full of comings and goings. Much as life went on at Crantock, thought Kelsie, painfully. Toby wasn't at Crantock – but he wasn't here, either. The still child in the bed wasn't Toby. Tears began to slide down her face.

Suddenly, Mrs Lanyon gripped her hand and said in a voice more like her usual self.

'Kelsie, love, go home now. Get Roger to give you a hot toddy and go to bed. Don't visit again until Toby's come round. The doctors are confident it will be soon – really they are. They thought there was some improvement today.' She signalled briskly to

Roger and he led Kelsie from the ward, blind with tears.

It had been nearly a week since the accident. As they came through the front door at Crantock, Kelsie noticed the date on the 'Horse and Hound' calendar by the telephone. It was circled in felt-tip pen, but Kelsie's tired brain could not remember why. She saw that the hall table was thick with dust and there was a vase of long-dead flowers on it. Suddenly she shivered. Roger noticed.

'It's gone cooler. Perhaps there'll be a break in the weather at last.' They could hear a clatter of activity from the direction of the kitchen. 'Someone's still here. Mrs Patterson said they'd be gone by the time we got back.' Roger was surprised. 'I wonder if they've re-lit the Rayburn. It's been out for two days now.'

Just then the kitchen door opened, letting a stream of warm light into the hall. Standing in the doorway was Kelsie's mother.

'Hello, you two,' she said. 'I guessed you'd be at the hospital. Supper's ready.'

'Oh, Mum!' Kelsie was filled with remorse. 'I forgot you were arriving today. There was no one to meet you at the station.'

'That's all right, dear. I got your letter about Toby so I knew you'd all be at sixes and sevens – and I can afford a taxi these days! Now come on in to the kitchen and tell me how he is.'

Roger eyed the table appreciatively. They hadn't sat down to a proper meal since the previous weekend, and it looked as if Mrs Forbes had used her initiative in raiding the store cupboard. He drew up a chair.

'There's no real change, I'm afraid,' he began. The telephone rang.

'I'll go,' said Kelsie wearily, but in a few moments she was back in the room, her face radiant.

'It was Jean . . . Toby regained consciousness ten minutes after we left!'

'Thank God,' said Roger, simply. The next few moments were a confusion of laughter, tears and hugging, with Ajax emerging from beneath the table to add his barking to the noise. Mrs Forbes was the first to recover and she insisted on their sitting down to the meal.

'For the first time I feel as if I could eat. Although it's not all over yet.' Kelsie's face clouded again. 'I mean, we still don't know that Toby's going to recover completely. Didn't they say there was some spinal injury?'

'Stop it, Kelsie.' Roger was at the dresser opening a bottle of elderberry wine. 'We're going to eat, drink and be merry and take tomorrow as it comes. So do as you're told and sit down.'

'Yes, sir,' said Kelsie meekly and looked at him with the ghost of a grin. But when they raised their glasses in a toast to Toby's recovery, she couldn't help glancing at the three empty places at the table.

9

Detective Work

Later that evening, Mr and Mrs Lanyon came home. Mrs Lanyon was so exhausted that she could hardly put two words together, so she was bustled off to bed by Mrs Forbes in a sisterly fashion. Kelsie was cheered to see her drop an unopened packet of cigarettes in the bin as she left the room. Meanwhile Mr Lanyon told Roger and Kelsie more about Toby.

'He's a bit confused – doesn't remember the accident, I'm afraid. And he was a bit panicky because he couldn't move his legs.' Kelsie's stomach gave a sudden lurch, but Mr Lanyon went on quickly, 'The doctor hopes it's a temporary paralysis and they'll begin physiotherapy straight away. He's asleep now, and comfortable. He'll be moved down to the children's ward tomorrow and he asked if he could see you as soon as possible. I can hold the fort here if you want to go in in the morning.'

As Kelsie got ready for bed, the relief she had felt because Toby had come round was replaced by the new anxiety that Murphy might have crippled him for life . . . Toby, who she had always thought destined for a career in show-jumping, Toby, so full of life and activity, to be confined to a wheelchair like poor Jimmy and Douglas?

She crawled into bed, too miserably weary to cry, and fell into a fitful sleep, oppressed by indistinctly menacing dreams.

The rain was falling in torrents as Roger drove through the streets of Penloe.

'Thank heaven for the rain. We really needed it,' he commented. They had left Crantock with his parents still asleep, Mrs Forbes embarked on an orgy of housework, and Janet and Jane bustling about the puddle-filled stable yard with cheerful competence. Kelsie's spirits rose as they parked by the hospital. Perhaps Toby would be able to move his legs by now. Perhaps he would have remembered how the accident happened, and that terrible hurdle would be over.

Toby looked much better, as he sat propped up in bed at one end of the busy children's ward. It was comforting to see him surrounded by other children and free of the drip and monitors of the intensive care unit. His greeting was characteristic.

'Hi, you two. How's Firecracker?'

Roger pulled up a chair and reassured his brother that Firecracker was fine, though under-exercised.

'He's missing me.' Toby looked at Kelsie. 'He'll get awfully bad-tempered out of his routine. Could you spend some time on him?'

'Of course.' Kelsie came to the other side of the bed.

'It won't be for long. I'll be home soon and riding him myself.' There was a dangerous little crack in his voice and his eyes were unnaturally bright. Hastily, Roger changed the subject.

'Look, we're not allowed to stay long – the sister said you were due for physiotherapy. Can you tell us if you've remembered anything about the accident? It's rather important that Kelsie knows. If Murphy's dangerous, he ought to be put down.'

Kelsie looked intently at Toby, but he was staring at his brother in surprise.

'I was on Murphy, was I?'

'Yes,' Roger assured him. 'You went up on the Carn to take photographs and borrowed Murphy because the others were supposed to be resting.' Kelsie said nothing, willing Toby to remember.

'Oh.' Toby digested the information. 'I *think* I remember taking Murphy. No saddle, and the tatty old bridle, not his circus one. I remember putting the camera round my neck . . . and as we went up the lane I remember noticing how good Murphy had got with gates . . .' Kelsie nodded encouragingly, but Toby closed his eyes, looking suddenly tired.

'That's it. I don't remember any more.' He opened his eyes again. 'What happened to my camera?' he demanded. 'Was it broken?'

'The camera?' Roger was startled. 'I don't know.' He looked at Kelsie across the bed. 'Was it round his neck when you found him?'

Kelsie thought. She remembered the hikers removing the pile of jackets just before the ambulance men had covered him with the blanket. There had been no camera.

'We'll go and look for it,' promised Roger. 'We must go now. There's a lady in a white jacket and black trousers bearing down on you with a determined look in her eye.'

'The physio!' hissed Toby. 'I'm asleep!' He once more closed his eyes and Kelsie and Roger tip-toed away from the bed as if anxious not to disturb him. It was a useless ploy. The physiotherapist greeted her patient with a hearty cry of 'Wakey! Wakey! Time for a little exercise, young man!'

As they went through the door, Roger turned to Kelsie with a smile.

'They'll soon jolly him on to his feet. He'll be running round the ward to get away from her by the end of the week.'

'I hope so!' said Kelsie, anxiously. Roger stopped and looked at her. Then he grabbed her arm and hustled her down the corridor.

'Come on, let's get out of this place. I want to talk to you on the way home.'

Once in the car, Roger gave Kelsie a little lecture. She was to stop blaming herself for the accident immediately. It was no more her fault than anyone else's. Toby was an experienced rider and there had been no reason to suppose that Murphy was a naturally vicious horse.

'We'd all ridden him, even Dad,' Roger reminded her. 'He was even accepting the ordinary saddle. Anyway, don't forget that the best-behaved of horses is capable of throwing a rider if it's given a bad fright . . . so you must get rid of all these guilt feelings.' He paused, and looking straight at the road ahead, he added, 'Anyway, I have a hunch that it's possible Murphy had nothing to do with the accident.'

'*What?*' Kelsie's voice was a mixture of incredulity and hope.

'There's quite a lot that just doesn't add up. And I've a feeling that it's something to do with the camera.' Roger negotiated the flooded ruts of Crantock's lane. 'And after the last ride today, you and I are going to do a little detective work.'

By five o'clock the rain had eased off and Roger and Kelsie rode Sorrel and Firecracker up to the Carn. Firecracker was very lively, not having been ridden for over a week and seemed eager to gallop across the moorland in the direction of Land's End. They turned down to the Canyon, however, and dismounted, tying the horses to a gnarled and ancient thorn-tree by the track. The granite rocks glistened with wetness and the sky was still overcast. Kelsie buttoned up her jacket.

'It's quite cold. The summer's really over.' She felt sad. It had been a busy, but lovely summer at Crantock, the first she had spent here as one of the family instead of a holidaymaker. Why did it have to end with Toby's future in the balance? And Murphy's future. She concentrated on the matter in hand. Roger was walking along the path between the rocky walls, searching the ground. She ran to join him.

'If the camera was along here, someone would have found it by now.'

'Probably.' Roger looked up from his task. 'If it had been anywhere near Toby, one of those hikers would have picked it up and given it to you.'

'They seemed a responsible crowd. They wouldn't have walked off with it.' Kelsie was certain.

'Perhaps they were too excited to notice it. In

which case, if it was close to Toby, it would have been on the path and the next person to come along would have seen it.'

'It had Toby's name and address on the strap.'

'Some people aren't too honest . . . On the other hand, perhaps the camera *didn't* fall on to the path. In fact, I just don't see why it wasn't still round his neck, if Murphy threw him as they were coming through the Canyon.'

'It's an odd place for Murphy to have decided to throw a fit.' The thought had suddenly occurred to Kelsie. 'He's never shown the least dislike of enclosed spaces – not like Sorrel! And if he'd bucked or reared in here, he could have hurt himself.' Her voice echoed among the boulders.

'I checked him over the next morning,' said Roger, thoughtfully. 'Not a scratch on him. Come on, let's take a look round the other side.' He led the way out of the Canyon, and as they picked their way through the wet bracken, Kelsie remembered something else.

'*Toby* was covered in bruises and scratches – almost as if he'd been dragged along the ground. But there was no stirrup to catch his foot in.'

'I wonder . . .' Roger looked up at one side of the towering rock formation. 'Kelsie, suppose . . . just suppose Toby had decided to climb up to what we used to call the look-out. You remember, where we used to post whoever was the Indian scout.' Kelsie nodded. 'After all, he told you he wanted to take some sunset pictures, and you can see westwards across Penloe bay from up there. Let's climb up and take a look.'

It was a slippery scramble, but one that

generations of children had made and there were plenty of well-worn footholds. Once at the top, the two friends ignored the view and began to look among the cracks and hollows of the rock.

It was Kelsie who found the camera, a few feet below the flat surface of the look-out post, but away from the point where they had clambered up. It was half-hidden by brambles. Kelsie found that she was shaking all over, so Roger lowered himself down to retrieve the camera. It was damp and slightly scratched, but otherwise seemed undamaged. Roger re-joined Kelsie. They were now standing on a narrow ridge connecting the look-out post with the rest of the rock outcrop that made up one wall of the Canyon. Roger gently turned Kelsie around to look down at the pathway.

'Where did you find Toby?' he asked quietly.

Kelsie's mouth was dry.

'Just down there,' she whispered. 'Below us.'

'Sit down,' ordered Roger, immediately. 'We don't want *you* falling into the Canyon.' She did as she was told and put her head between her knees for a few moments. It made her feel less dizzy and she was able to attend to what Roger was saying. It seemed that he was convinced that Toby had stood exactly where they were now sitting. For some reason he had stumbled or stepped back and fallen down into the Canyon, 'collecting bruises, grazes, a crack on the head and a bang on the spine on the way,' guessed Roger. 'Just as he fell, he dropped the camera and it bounced in the opposite direction down to where we found it.' Kelsie swallowed hard.

'And Murphy?'

'Murphy had nothing to do with it.' Roger was emphatic. 'I've felt it in my bones ever since I started to wonder about the camera. I must admit I thought he was the culprit until then – though I wasn't going to let Jane bully you into having him destroyed when we had no proof.'

Kelsie carefully got to her feet.

'If you're right . . . and we don't know absolutely for sure . . . where was Murphy while this was going on?'

'Aha, my dear Watson, another flash of inspiration. Back to the thorn tree!'

His light-heartedness was infectious, and Kelsie slid down after him as fast as she could. Roger, with his long legs, reached the startled horses well ahead of her, and ran around the tree. As she breathlessly caught up, he gave a whoop of triumph. Instantly Kelsie was reminded again of those long-ago games of Cowboys and Indians. Roger looked as young as Toby, and his grin stretched from ear to ear.

'Found it!' He held aloft a broken branch in triumph. 'Toby tethered Murphy here, too. When Murphy realized something was up and Toby wasn't coming back, he pulled free, breaking the old reins and the branch!'

'Guesswork.' Kelsie wanted to be convinced, wanted to know for sure.

'Of course it's guesswork,' said Roger impatiently, adding in his Sherlock Holmes voice, 'but intelligent guesswork.' He slung Toby's camera round his neck and mounted Sorrel. 'The proof, my dear Watson,' he told Kelsie, tapping the camera, 'is in here!'

Roger emerged, bleary-eyed, from Toby's dark-room at half-past ten that night, a clutch of damp photographs in his hand. He paused on the lower landing and listened. Everyone seemed to be in the sitting-room. It was cool and raining again, so Mrs Forbes had lit a fire. Kelsie's mother had been amazing, thought Roger. She had simply walked in and taken over the running of the house, which was just as well, as the rota system had completely broken down, what with all the extra work and hospital visiting. Ellen Forbes, the darling of millions of TV viewers, was wielding a Hoover and producing relays of substantial meals as if she had been housekeeping for an army all her life. But underneath her cheerful calm, Roger had detected her concern about Kelsie's present state of mind. Perhaps these prints would reassure them both.

He walked into the sitting-room and dropped the photographs on Kelsie's lap.

'Here you are,' he said casually. 'Look at them in order.' The first four prints were of various groups of rocks silhouetted against the sky. Toby had obviously been aiming for dramatic effects in his sunset pictures. The fifth picture was of a view looking towards the bay and taken from the narrow part of the look-out post. The sixth picture was a blur of rock and sky.

'That was the last one. He must have pressed the button as he overbalanced.' Roger took the photos and handed them to his parents, who looked at them carefully and passed them on to Kelsie's mother. All seemed quite genuinely agreed that Roger's theory was more than likely. Kelsie looked from face to face. Yes, they really thought so. No one was pretending in order to make her feel better.

It was only now that she allowed herself to believe it too. Immediately she was filled with a new guilt. Murphy was all alone in the top field, unvisited, unwanted, unloved. She rushed for the door. Mrs Forbes sat up, bewildered.

'Where is she going at this time of night?'

'To see Murphy,' guessed Roger as the back door slammed. 'Kelsie's got an apology to make.'

'Murphy . . . Mur-phy!' called Kelsie through the rainy dark. It was a steep climb to the top field and she was out of breath. There was a distant neigh and she flashed her torch into the gloom. She could hear the muffled thud of hooves and the beam of light suddenly picked out the skewbald's white markings as he trotted towards her. He came to a halt and gave her his usual hello – a friendly butt in the chest, his great rain-streaked head dipped towards her pockets.

Murphy seemed to bear no ill-will for being neglected, and after accepting two apples and a Polo, he nuzzled her gently, in an affectionate manner, not asking for more. Kelsie leaned against him and stroked his shoulder. In the darkness she felt, rather than saw, him make one of his dreadful faces.

'You're a horror,' she whispered lovingly. 'But I wouldn't change you now. Not for anything.'

Kelsie resumed Murphy's training straight away, once again spending every spare moment with him. Now as she rode him confidently over track and moorland, she no longer thought regretfully of the 'might-have-been' dream horse.

Meanwhile October came, bringing more rain and wild weather with it, and Toby began to improve. Gradually sensation was returning to his legs and the physiotherapist was confident that he would soon be on his feet. There was talk of him coming home soon and receiving treatment as an out-patient, which cheered him up considerably.

There was a constant stream of visitors to his end of the ward. Janet managed a visit after school every day, and Toby's bed often seemed surrounded by friends from his class or the Pony Club.

A sensation was caused in the ward the day that Kelsie's mother first came to see Toby. It just so happened that nearly everyone was watching the latest episode of 'Pringle's Parish'. The credits were rolling as Mrs Forbes walked into the ward with Kelsie. Children and nurses all stared at her, unable to believe their eyes.

'It's Bella Pringle!' squeaked a little girl in red pyjamas, pointing excitedly. Thereupon, Mrs Forbes had to make a tour of the whole ward, talking to everyone and signing autographs.

'It's like a Royal Progress,' sighed Kelsie, sitting beside Toby. 'You know she has to wear a headscarf and dark glasses just to go shopping in Penloe? It's awful . . . Sorry, Toby. She's not going to have much time for you.'

'That's all right.' Toby sat in a wheelchair next to the bed of a boy with his leg in heavy plaster. 'Meet my friend, Jason. His plaster's coming off tomorrow.'

'Wouldn't they let you home with your leg in plaster?' Kelsie was sympathetic.

'No, they wouldn't trust me not to go and break the other one. I'm always breaking things.' Jason seemed totally unconcerned about this situation.

'How did you break your leg.'

'Grass-skiing.' Jason gave a shout of laughter. 'I'll try anything once. Football, gymnastics, trampoline . . .' The three youngsters chatted for a while until Kelsie decided it was time to rescue her mother.

'Come on, Toby, let's remind her she's here to see you.' Toby swung the wheelchair into the middle of the ward. 'I like your friend Jason,' Kelsie remarked. 'He seems to have a great sense of humour.' Toby grinned smugly.

'You didn't even notice, did you?'

'Notice what?'

'Jason's blind.'

'And he broke his leg *skiing*?' Kelsie was astounded, but her attention was distracted from the amazing Jason by her mother disengaging herself from her admirers and coming towards them full of apologies.

'I'm so sorry, they all wanted to ask about the show – I couldn't get away.'

'I can't imagine why they like it,' Toby informed her. 'I think it's awfully boring.' Mrs Forbes looked at him seriously.

'Do you know, so do I!'

'I like some television though,' Toby went on blithely. 'There's a good thriller on in five minutes.' He steered the wheelchair towards the set. Kelsie and her mother smiled at one another and made for the ward exit.

'I can't exactly say I've visited Toby,' mused Mrs Forbes. 'I'll try again tomorrow, before I catch my train.'

Mrs Forbes's holiday was over. She had worked wonders with the Crantock domestic arrangements, brushing aside all protests.

'This *is* a holiday for me. It's been great fun catering for all of you instead of returning to a lonely little flat, where it takes no time at all to produce a meal for one.' Everyone was sorry to see her go, but she promised to return soon.

'Probably before Christmas. I've a few things to sort out; arrangements to make, but I hope to be able to spend more time here in Cornwall very soon.'

Kelsie would have been rather sad, seeing her mother off at the station, if the Lanyons had not had good news from the hospital that morning. Toby was walking, with help, it was true, but it looked as if his recovery would be complete, and that he would be allowed home at the end of the week.

Toby's homecoming became quite a party. Various friends turned up at Crantock during the day to welcome him. A television had arrived that morning and had been installed in the study, which had been turned into a temporary bedroom for Toby, to avoid his having to negotiate all the stairs to the attic. The portable set was a present from Mrs

Forbes, as a compensation for being housebound for a while. She had also left an elaborate cake, decorated with a miniature show-jumper and Kelsie and Janet had hung a 'Welcome Home, Toby' banner over the front door and had festooned the hall with streamers and balloons.

Callers had been phoning and arriving all day, so it was no surprise when, just as Toby was cutting the cake, there was a ring of the front door-bell. Kelsie was near the dining-room door.

'I'll go,' she called over the din. She swung back the old oak door. There on the doorstep stood Tara, in an expensive-looking coat with a fur collar. Behind her was an estate car and a horse-box.

'I've come to collect Murphy,' she said.

10

'Murphy's Mine!'

Tara smiled as she stepped into the hall. Kelsie shut the door after her, speechless with astonishment. Roger was standing by the dining-room door and had obviously heard Tara's bombshell.

'You've got a nerve,' he said quietly but emphatically. Tara was brought up short.

'I beg your pardon?'

'You heard.'

Kelsie had rarely seen Roger so angry. As the shock of the circus girl's unexpected arrival wore off, she too began to feel an overwhelming anger. How could Tara march in and take Murphy away – just when he'd been proved reliable, just when she had discovered how fond of him she'd grown. She clenched her fists at her sides and prepared to join the verbal battle, but found it was a one-sided contest. Tara was staring open-mouthed at Roger while he berated her with stinging coolness.

'Moreover,' he finished, sounding very much like his father on a bad day, 'may I remind you that Kelsie still has your high-handed letter in which you so graciously say "please consider Murphy your property from now on". I think that's a pretty conclusive statement, don't you?'

Kelsie felt like applauding. If they must hand over Murphy – and the very thought made her shake with fury – they wouldn't do so without a fight.

Tara looked from one to the other, her dark eyes wide with disbelief.

'You want to keep him?' she said, incredulously.

'*Yes!*' cried Kelsie, fiercely. 'I've cared for him, and schooled him . . . and loved him. This is his home now, and you can't have him back. Murphy's mine!' She turned to Roger, who looked calmer now, as he leaned against the door with his hands in his pockets.

'There's no question of Tara having him back. He's yours, Kelsie, that letter proves it.'

Suddenly Tara laughed, and sat on the edge of the hall table.

'And I thought I was doing you a favour! I don't want Murphy back.' Now it was Kelsie's turn to stare.

'But you just said you'd come for him!'

'I know, but that was when I thought you would be only too pleased to get rid of him. My conscience has been pricking me ever since I left for Switzerland. I was so anxious that Dad would try to stop me and I was pretty desperate to find somewhere for Murphy quickly. It was only later that I realized how sneaky I'd been, not giving you a chance to say no. Specially as you were obviously conscientious types and would probably keep him.' Tara smiled, and Kelsie felt herself begin to smile back. Perhaps it was going to be all right after all . . . 'Anyway,' continued Tara, 'I'm back in England for a few weeks to record the act for a Christmas circus for the BBC and I thought I'd drop by and take Murphy off your hands. The Cirque de

Zurich are getting together a rodeo act and he might have been useful.' Tara shrugged her elegant shoulders. 'As it is, I'm sure he'll be better off here. You're riding him, did you say? With a saddle?'

Relief loosened Kelsie's tongue. As she began to recount all the adventures of the summer, Roger slipped into the dining-room once more. His mother soon appeared in the hall to invite Tara to join the family celebration. Once he realized that Murphy was to stay, Toby was pleased to see her and eager to ask questions about Princess. Immediately Tara was in her element, describing her new life as a star of an international circus to the Lanyons and their friends. It was quite late when at last her car swept up the lane on its way to Penloe's grandest hotel.

Kelsie breathed an enormous sigh of relief as she shut the front door. She looked at Mrs Lanyon.

'She's gone. And she didn't even ask to see Murphy. Oh Lord, I hope she doesn't ever change her mind again.' Suddenly she felt very weary. It had been an emotional day, what with Toby's homecoming and Tara's visit. It was strange how the threat of losing Murphy had made him seem so precious.

Mrs Lanyon put her arm through Kelsie's and walked with her towards the kitchen.

'Don't you worry, I don't think we shall see that young lady again, unless it's on the television at Christmas . . . Talking of television . . .' Mrs Lanyon stopped and opened the study door. 'Switch that set off immediately, Toby, and go to sleep. You're still supposed to be an invalid, remember?' There was no reply. Toby was fast asleep, with 'Match of the Day' blaring at full volume.

So far it had been a typical Cornish winter, mild but wet, and Crantock had to be flexible with its RDA sessions. There had been several indoor lessons on tack-cleaning and stable management, which had usually developed into lively social occasions as well. All the helpers felt that time wasn't wasted in this way, and that it was better than cancelling the visits.

Mrs Lanyon often looked forward to the day when they could expand the Methion branch's activities, but for the moment she felt that they had as many riders as they could cope with. There was one new rider, however, that everyone was only too happy to make room for, for the very good reason that he was brought to them by Toby.

For some time now, Mrs Lanyon had been pleased to find Toby turning up to some of the indoor sessions. He was not allowed to ride just yet, and even the television had begun to pall and so possibly he was just killing time. However, one Monday afternoon, the week before he was due to start school again, Toby told his mother that he would like to be a regular helper.

'It isn't just that I want to get time off school,' he explained, looking rather pink and avoiding his mother's eyes. 'It's just that . . . well, when I was lying in that hospital bed and thinking that I might never ride again, or at best be a handicapped rider like Jimmy, needing helpers all the time, I thought . . .' Toby paused and looked down at the saddle he was so carefully polishing.

'Go on,' prompted Mrs Lanyon gently.

'I thought I'd rather ride with that kind of help than not ride at all.' Toby lifted his head and looked straight at his mother. 'It's really weird, I would never have thought I'd feel like that. I would have thought it would be all or nothing . . . Anyway, that's why I want to help now, do you see?'

'Of course I do.'

'Don't tell the others what I've just said. It sounds awfully goody-goody.'

Mrs Lanyon laughed.

'Bless you, Toby, I won't if you don't want me to – but I don't think there's much chance of you being mistaken for a saint yet awhile!'

And then Toby had produced Jason. The boy's mother had driven him to Crantock one Monday afternoon and Toby had led him into the stable office with the air of a conjurer pulling a rabbit out of a hat.

'This is Jason,' he announced proudly. 'He's tried everything except riding.'

'And broken nearly everything, too,' put in Jason.

'You're not breaking anything *here*,' stated Toby, sternly, 'because I shall be in charge of you – can I be, Mum?' He added his request so pleadingly that Mrs Lanyon hadn't the heart to protest that they really shouldn't take any more riders at present. Anyway, she had some rather good ideas for blind riders that she was longing to try out.

As might have been expected, Jason turned out to be quite a handful, but as far as Mrs Lanyon was concerned that was more than compensated for by Toby's presence in the RDA classes. With everyone at Crantock now behind it, the scheme could only go from strength to strength. She and Kelsie often planned for the future – more disabled riders, some joining in with the ordinary pupils' classes, an indoor school if they could ever raise the money, even an RDA gymkhana. Mrs Lanyon remembered Toby's blindfold jumping at the Pony Club. Perhaps it hadn't been such a pointless trick after all. Perhaps Jason would one day be jumping – it could be done! It was going to continue to be hard work of course, but if Ellen Forbes went ahead with the plans she had been making, then some areas of life at Crantock could get a lot easier.

It was Christmas morning, and Roger, Kelsie and Toby were taking their traditional before-lunch ride up on the Carn. It was clear and frosty, but Kelsie felt warm with a glow of satisfaction. Roger glanced at his friend and thought that she looked like an illustration from a Christmas card in her grey habit and the jaunty top hat with the little veil that had been a present from her mother. It was a pity that her mount spoiled the illusion. Murphy, his thick winter coat ruffled like a hearthrug, plodded up the hill ahead of Sorrel with all the grace of an army tank.

In the lead, Firecracker bounced along, the nip in the air making him eager for a gallop, but the ground was iron-hard and Toby was keeping him well in hand.

It was marvellous to see Toby riding again, thought Kelsie. The last few weeks had been very relaxed, after the anxieties of the autumn. Jean Lanyon had spent a lot of time supervising Toby's riding, 'little and often' as the physiotherapist had recommended. She had been able to spend the time with Toby mainly thanks to Ellen Forbes. The inner glow became even warmer as Kelsie thought of her mother.

It was only after her departure after her hectic holiday, that Kelsie had remembered that they were supposed to have discussed the mysterious plans that her mother had once hinted at over the telephone. But life had been in such a turmoil with all the anxieties over Toby's accident, that somehow they had not been mentioned.

Then three weeks ago, without warning, Mrs Forbes had turned up at Crantock driving a large estate car from which she had unloaded an enormous quantity of luggage. All the Lanyons were engaged in carrying bags and suitcases into the house, when Mrs Forbes stopped to hug her daughter.

'Don't look so amazed, love. It isn't just Christmas presents. These are all my worldly goods. I've come to stay!'

'To stay?' Kelsie was bewildered. 'Do you mean for good?'

'I'll explain as soon as we've got everything inside.' She turned to Mrs Lanyon. 'Sorry to arrive earlier than you expected, Jean, but the news broke this morning and I had to get away before the press besieged the flat.'

'*What* news?' demanded Kelsie, but she had to wait for an answer.

Over tea, Mrs Forbes explained. She had left the cast of 'Pringle's Parish'. Only the day before she had recorded the episode in which Bella Pringle was tragically killed in a fire at the vicarage.

'I knew by this summer that I couldn't go on with it,' Ellen Forbes told them. 'It wasn't the work itself, that was quite fun. It was the way everyone expected me to *be* Bella all the time. I know some people seem to thrive on being recognized in the street and written about in the newspapers, but it's not a way of life that suits me. So back in October I told them I wanted to terminate my contract.'

'Didn't they mind?' asked Kelsie.

'Oh yes, they minded a lot at first – until the scriptwriters began to see how they could turn my departure to their advantage. Hence poor Bella Pringle's grisly end. You'll see, the ratings will shoot up after Christmas when that episode's shown.'

'So what are you going to do now?'

'Sorry, love, I'm afraid Jean and I have been making arrangements behind your back again, partly in case things didn't work out at the Manchester end. Anyway, I've made a lot of money this year, with the series and all the commercials I've made, so finances won't be a problem for a long time – there might even be a film part for me coming up next year. So Jean and I have agreed that Crantock will be my home too from now on, and that I am going to housekeep for you all while you get on with running the stables. If any TV or film work turns up, I'll take it, if it's something I really want to do, but I imagine that most of the time I'm going to be here with you.'

This was news that even now made Kelsie bubble with happiness. During the last year there had been many times when she had wished her mother wasn't so far away, and now her wish had come true.

At the top of the Carn the three friends had a brief argument about which way to go. Kelsie wanted to go on the track that circled the Three Sisters mines and came back through Crantock woods, but Roger thought it would take them too long.

'We can't go at much of a pace with the ground so hard, and your mother won't be best pleased if we spoil the dinner by being late.'

'They won't let it spoil,' Toby put in anxiously. 'They'll start without us, and that'll be just as bad.'

'Greedy-guts,' teased Kelsie. Toby regarded her coldly.

'I should put that veil right down if I were you. It'll be a great improvement.'

'Shut up, you two,' said Roger automatically. 'Which way *are* we going, then?'

'Through the Canyon and home again by the road. The road will have thawed by now and we can trot.'

'OK, Toby. Lead on.'

The horses picked their way down towards the rocks. They paused for a moment in the Canyon to look up at the sheer walls.

'Golly,' said Toby in a subdued tone. 'Fancy falling all that way.' He turned to look at Kelsie. 'You know, I remember standing up on the top taking photos, now, but I still don't remember falling – and I'm jolly glad I don't.'

'I shouldn't dwell on it.' Roger was brisk. 'It's you that's so worried about being late for the turkey, so get a move on.'

Once on the road, Kelsie put unhappy reminders of the accident behind her. As Murphy went into his ungainly trot, she thought of their early-morning visit to the Pattersons' bungalow. It had been one of the best Christmassy things they had ever done, she decided, helping to play Santa Claus to Janet Patterson.

For Mrs Patterson, thanks to Crantock and the RDA, had been quite won over to the idea of Janet having a pony and had enlisted the help of the Lanyons in choosing and buying a Highland pony as close to Butterscotch in size and character as they could find. He had been delivered to Crantock and kept there over Christmas Eve. Then at an appointed time after breakfast, Kelsie and Toby had taken the pony over to Methion village and the Pattersons'. Just as they led him up the drive, an unsuspecting Janet had been brought to the door. The expression on her face as she saw the pony was one that Kelsie would never forget.

Murphy was last through the farm gate, mainly because he outshone both Sorrel and Firecracker at gate-shutting. Kelsie patted his neck and turned him down the last stretch of track to the stables. He was turning out to be quite a gentleman despite his uncouth appearance. Dear old Murphy. No – not old, of course. He was still very young. There was still a lot for him, and her, to learn. They would learn it together. Somehow Kelsie knew that she and Murphy, the ugly skewbald that no one had wanted, were just entering a very happy partnership.

JOKE BOOKS

If you're an eager Beaver reader, perhaps you ought to try some more of our hilarious Beaver joke books. They are available in bookshops or they can be ordered directly from us. Just complete the form below and enclose the right amount of money and the books will be sent to you at home.

	Title	Author	Price
☐	THE BROWNIE JOKE BOOK	Brownies	95p
☐	MORE BROWNIE JOKES	Brownies	95p
☐	JELLYBONE GRAFFITI BOOK	Therese Birch	95p
☐	SCHOOL GRAFFITI	Peter Eldin	95p
☐	SKOOL FOR LAUGHS	Peter Eldin	95p
☐	THE WOOLLY JUMPER JOKE BOOK	Peter Eldin	95p
☐	THE FUNNIEST JOKE BOOK	Jim Eldridge	£1.00
☐	THE WOBBLY JELLY JOKE BOOK	Jim Eldridge	95p
☐	HOW TO HANDLE GROWN-UPS	Jim Eldridge	£1.00
☐	THE CRAZY JOKER'S HANDBOOK	Janet Rogers	£1.00
☐	THE CRAZY JOKE BOOK STRIKES BACK	Janet Rogers	£1.00
☐	THE ELEPHANT JOKE BOOK	Katie Wales	£1.00
☐	FALL ABOUT WITH FLO	Floella Benjamin	£1.25

And if you would like to hear more about Beaver Books, and find out all the latest news, don't forget the BEAVER BULLETIN. Just send a stamped, self-addressed envelope to Beaver Books, 62 – 65 Chandos Place, Covent Garden, London WC2N 4NW.

If you would like to order books, please send this form, and the money due to:

HAMLYN PAPERBACK CASH SALES, PO BOX 11, FALMOUTH, CORNWALL TR10 9EN.

Send a cheque or postal order, and don't forget to include postage at the following rates: UK: 55p for first book, 22p for the second, 14p thereafter; BFPO and Eire: 55p for first book, 22p for the second, 14p per copy for next 7 books, 8p per book thereafter; Overseas £1.00 for first book, 25p thereafter.

NAME..

ADDRESS..

....

Please print clearly